Fleabag and the Ring's

The wizards of Porthwain are challenging the
Ring Fire – by strength, wisdom and magic.
Gemma the Fire Wielder and King Phelan
must defeat the perilous Blue Magic, or lose
the Kingdom.

But Gemma believes the Ring Fire cannot be
used like magic, even to win this battle. Will the
warrior princess Rowanne fight the wizards on
her behalf, or has Rowanne become a pawn of the
Blue Magic? Where is the Ring's End? And who
is Kern, the mysterious fiddle-player?

Only Fleabag the cat, Gemma's protector and
the wiliest adviser on three legs in the Kingdom,
knows the answers. And he's not telling…

Beth Webb lives in Somerset with her four
children and an entourage of pets. Her first two
books in this series are *Fleabag and the Ring Fire*
and *Fleabag and the Fire Cat*. Her other books for
children include *The Magic in the Pool of Making*,
The Witch of Wookey Hole and *Foxdown Wood*.

For Michael Collins,
also for Lynn – and Francis,
who makes me larf!

Fleabag and the Ring's End

Beth Webb

LION
Children's Books

Copyright © 2000 Beth Webb

The author asserts the moral right
to be identified as the author of this work

Published by
Lion Publishing
Sandy Lane West, Oxford, England
www.lion-publishing.co.uk
ISBN 0 7459 4411 6

First edition 2000
10 9 8 7 6 5 4 3 2 1 0

All rights reserved

Acknowledgments
My special thanks to Saoirse, the wonderful singer and
musician of the 'Isolde's Tower', Dublin, who gave me
the character of Kern/Saoirse.
Thanks, as usual, to Su Box and Sarah Hall for their
patience and perseverance.
Also to Mum and Dad who are always so encouraging!

A catalogue record for this book is available
from the British Library

Typeset in 11/12.5 Aldine
Printed and bound in Great Britain by
Omnia Books Ltd, Scotland

Contents

1

The Fiddle Player

The boy bent his head over the fiddle and lifted the bow across the strings. Then, with a small jerk of his right shoulder, the music began.

The notes ran so fast and furious everyone in the market place stopped to listen.

Stallholders let onions fall back into boxes, and old women stopped their gossiping. Children who had been about to steal apples forgot what they were doing and squatted on the stone cobbles to listen.

Time seemed to have stopped as the thin-faced boy played on and on. The crowd grew silently bigger and bigger as the spinning notes filled the air.

At first he played jigs and reels and merry dance tunes, then almost imperceptibly the melodies became slower and sadder, until at last he dropped his arms and let the bow and fiddle dangle between his thin fingers. After a moment he put his head back, closed his eyes, and sang a sweet, yearning air.

When he stopped there was a long, long silence.

Then just as suddenly as the seeming spell had been cast, it was broken. With one voice, the whole crowd roared its approval and burst into thunderous applause. The boy was showered with coins and fruit and small gifts as, one by one, the listeners went about their business.

The little musician bent to pack up his things and to gather his earnings into a basket. When he straightened again he was alone – except, that is, for a mangy, black, long-haired cat, who was staring at him with golden eyes.

'What do you want, cat?' the boy sneered.

'Nothing,' the cat replied, as he scratched at a passing flea. 'I just wondered…'

'Yes?'

'I just wondered what your fiddle strings were made of.'

'Cat gut,' the boy said, snapping the locks of the violin case shut.

'Hmmm,' the cat grunted disapprovingly, as he pulled himself up stiffly onto three legs. 'Do you want a job playing for the evening? You'd be paid and given somewhere to sleep.'

The boy slung his basket over his shoulder and tucked his fiddle under his arm. It was a bitterly cold day, and the night would be worse. He was tempted. But he had his orders, and the sooner it was all over the better. 'No. I don't play for performing animals,' he sniffed. 'I'm after real work.'

'Suit yourself!' The cat twitched his whiskers as he turned to go. But just as he did so, the pale winter sunlight caught the glint of a large golden earring in his right ear.

The boy almost dropped everything. Could he have found his enemy so easily? He mustn't let him slip away. A three-legged rough-looking street cat with a golden earring? No, it must be some strange coincidence. But he had to find out.

'Just a moment,' he called, grabbing at the basket that swung from his shoulders as he ran. 'I'm sorry, I didn't mean to sound rude. My name is Kern. Where did you say you wanted me to play tonight?'

An hour later, the boy was eating bread and cheese in the servants' kitchen of the Royal Palace, seated by the warm fire. Fleabag and Kern watched each other intensely. The boy's fair straight hair was cut in an old-fashioned way, all the same length, framing a long, thin pale face with large grey-green eyes. Outwardly, there was nothing unusual about him, a wandering musician, probably from the West. He had extraordinary skill, it was true. The cat had an odd feeling in the tip of his tail about this lad.

But was it good or bad... or maybe both? Whatever it was, he wanted to keep him well within sight until he had put two and two together. The Battle of Spider Island had taught him to pay strict attention to funny feelings about strange visitors... at least until things were a bit clearer.

When Domnall the evil wizard had come, pretending to be nothing more than the Chancellor of the University of Porthwain, Fleabag had let him slip through his paws, and what terrible things had happened in consequence! Domnall had kidnapped Gemma the Fire Wielder and the Blue Magic had almost swamped everything. Now, this lad had more of a... well, of a *green* feeling to him than a blue one, but he still needed watching.

As he ate, the boy forgot his suspicions and concentrated on his food. At last, he pushed his wooden

9

trencher aside and leaned back in his chair contentedly.

'Finished?' Fleabag enquired kindly. 'Would you
like a tankard of nettle beer?'

The boy looked around. 'I would. Where is it?'

'I'll get it for you,' came a voice from behind the
kitchen door. Just then a tall, thin, freckle-faced
teenage girl walked in, surrounded by a sea of kittens, all mewing for their tea.

As soon as they saw their grandfather Fleabag,
they all swarmed around him until the cat was
drowned under a pile of soft balls of multicoloured
fur.

The girl drew two draughts of nettle beer and sat
down opposite the boy at the kitchen table. 'Hello,
I'm Gemma,' she introduced herself, smiling. 'Are
you a friend of Fleabag's?'

'Not really,' he blushed, already ashamed of his
deceit. 'I'm a musician. I met the cat while I was
busking in the market this afternoon. He asked me
to play at the Fire Festival tonight and I agreed.'

Gemma clapped her hands with delight.
'Excellent! Are you playing for the procession or for
the dancing afterwards?'

The boy blushed even more deeply. 'For the
dancing, I suppose. I... I don't know any of the Ring
Fire tunes. We don't play them where I come from,'
he added hastily.

'That's a shame. There're some great songs, and
my friend Phelan has a wonderful singing voice. I'll
introduce you to him later; perhaps you can work
out one or two melodies?'

He forced a smile. 'Thanks, I'd like that.' He had

no intention of learning his enemy's music, but if this girl and her friend could keep him in favour at the palace, he might be able to hang around long enough to work out a way of getting close to the King, and maybe even that terrible harridan, the Fire Wielder. If it meant he had to play a tune or two, what did that matter?

'Do you work here?' he asked as he wiped the nettle beer away from his mouth.

'Yes,' the girl laughed. 'I have my own home in the mountains near Beulothin, but I work here when I'm needed.'

'Rubbish!' scoffed Fleabag as he jumped up onto the table, having led his grand-kittens away to the scullery where the day's scraps had already been put down for them. 'Getting you to lift a finger to de-flea me takes far more effort than it should. I really will have to have words with the King about you!'

'Well, you shouldn't encourage the fleas. If you used flea powder and let the maids comb you every day, you'd have no trouble at all!'

Fleabag pounced suddenly on a wandering black speck and licked his whiskers. 'But fleas are so nice and *crunchy*, with that *hint* of sweetness in the middle... they're just... Ummm!'

Kern smiled. Despite himself, he couldn't help liking this creature. 'So are you in charge of the cat?'

Gemma threw back her head and laughed loudly. 'Ha!'

Fleabag jumped off the table and flicked his whiskers in mock annoyance. 'I'd like to see her try to be in charge of me. I'm in charge of *her*, more like! See you later. Nap time!' And with that he strode out of the kitchen, tail erect, followed, inevitably, by a few of the kittens, chasing and pouncing and clambering all around their granddad.

Gemma picked up the boy's dishes, washed them in the huge stone sink and left them to dry. 'I'll show you where you can have a bath and a chance to tune up before the Festival starts. Then I'll have to leave you to your own devices, I'm afraid. I've got to put an uncomfortable costume on and take part in the parade. But afterwards I'll make a special point of listening to you in the dance hall.'

Gemma led him up to the servants' quarters. No one was around. 'Everyone is over in the King's palace getting ready for tonight, but that cupboard over there has spare clothes for anyone who needs them, and the bathroom is here...' she pushed open a door to her left. 'Hal is the chief kitchen boy. Tell him Gemma asked him to look after you. I may not get a chance to speak to you later, but I hope all goes well.' And with that she smiled and ran back down the stairs and into the gardens that surrounded each of the palace buildings.

Just as she stepped outside onto the frosted gravel path, a husky voice behind her whispered 'Psst!' urgently.

'What's the matter, Fleabag?' She bent down and picked him up so she could scratch him under his chin.

'I don't trust him,' the cat growled.

'He seems a nice enough lad,' Gemma smiled. 'You're getting suspicious in your old age!'

'No. Seriously,' Fleabag answered, 'he uses *cat-gut* strings!'

2

The Blue Crystal

Kern pulled the clean shirt over his head and combed his hair. He did feel better for a bath, but he hated himself for liking Fleabag and his friend. She must be one of the higher servants at the palace, to be able to give Hal orders, but her plain linen dress and brown embroidered waistcoat looked like something a parlourmaid might wear on her day off. Perhaps she was just Fleabag's friend. Kern decided to be nice to her. She might be able to get him into all sorts of places and she might know some of the Fire Wielder's servants...

When Kern was dressed he sat at a small table at the end of the attic room. He placed the chair so he would have his back to anyone who came in. He had tried to shut the door, but it wouldn't catch properly. He daren't put something against it; that might look suspicious.

He opened his basket and from the end of his violin case pulled a small blue velvet bag. Carefully he pulled the laces apart and let a smooth blue crystal ball roll out onto his open hand. Then, placing it in front of him, he peered into it.

The clear blue stone shone with a chilly light that came from its heart; as he looked, he felt its cold pervading everywhere. He shivered, but did not dare look away. M'Kinnik, the chief wizard at Porthwain, would know if his mind wandered, and he would be punished with cramps all night.

Soon he felt the wizard's mind touching his own. 'I'm here, M'Kinnik. I'm in the palace, and I have been hired to play at the Festival tonight. I have already made the acquaintance of the cat, Fleabag, and a maid who seems friendly enough.

'I'm certain they are not suspicious. I will speak to you again as soon as I have more information for you.'

A chill crept between the boy's shoulderblades as he felt the cruel mind of the wizard threatening, 'And you know what will happen if you fail?'

'I know, Master.' The boy shivered, and put his hand over the ball to shield himself from its cruel blueness. How he longed to throw it as far out of the window as he could and walk away for ever. But too much was at stake.

Kern did not understand why the wizards of Porthwain wanted so badly to take over the Ring Fire and the Kingdom. They had already been defeated by the treacherous Fire Maiden at the Battle of Porthwain, and at the Battle of Spider Island. What was the point of trying again? All the wizards seemed to care about was making everyone do as they said. They were bullies, that was all.

True, Kern had his own reasons for agreeing to be the wizards' emissary. He longed to get his own back on the Fire Maiden. After the Battle of Porthwain she had become the Fire Wielder, which probably made her the Ring Fire's own all-powerful chief wizard. It was said she had more authority than the King, and if you looked her in the eye, you would shrivel up in an instant. She had been responsible for the death of his father, the Chancellor of All Wizards, and his two older brothers, Sethan and Domnall.

He wasn't worried by the death of his father or Sethan. They had never had any time for him, but he missed Domnall.

If Kern had been a girl things would have been different. She would have been his third daughter, and in wizard families, the third girl was usually the most powerful magician of all. But he already had the six sons he needed for his spells, so Kern was of no use to him. It was not good to be a wizard's seventh brat.

Besides, his father had been horrid to Claire, his mother. She was one of the Hill People, and had grown up on a farm owned by the University. When her father became too poor to pay the rent, Claire was taken instead. A fortune-teller had foreseen that this girl would give birth to an extraordinarily powerful daughter. The Chancellor already had several wives, and he hated Claire on sight, but he tolerated her until the baby was born. When he saw it was a boy, Claire was sent to work in the kitchens. Neither Sethan nor their father had looked at Kern since.

Domnall, on the other hand, had always been at least a little kind to Kern. When he was younger Domnall had given him sweets and outgrown clothes, and had taught him to read and to say a few simple spells. Kern was good at the reading, although he didn't like the spells. He only learned them to please his older brother.

And it had been Domnall who had given him his first violin...

Then Domnall too became Chancellor of All Wizards, and in his turn was killed by the Fire Wielder. Kern hated her for that. When his work for the wizards was done, he would avenge himself on the woman. She had killed the only person in all the world who meant anything to him, apart from his mother, and it was his mother who would suffer most if Kern failed.

He didn't dare think about it. He must concentrate on playing well at the Festival tonight. That would ensure that he would be allowed to hang around the palace until he found who he was looking for...

As he put the crystal ball back in his basket and pulled out his violin, Kern thought he saw a flicker of a dark shadow by the door. He looked again, but it was nothing. He rested the fiddle under his chin and began to tune up.

Meanwhile Fleabag sat outside in the corridor and thought hard. Had the boy seen him slipping out through the doorway? Well, what if he had? He was only a cat, and cats wandered everywhere. But what had Kern been doing with that crystal ball? Maybe nothing. It was probably only a glass bauble he had picked up on a market stall.

But the cat was beginning to feel increasingly uneasy...

Just then Hal came thumping up the stairs,

followed by a gaggle of other lads his own age. He stopped to stroke Fleabag and pushed the door wide open.

'Hello,' he called out cheerfully. 'Are you Kern? Gemma said I'd find you here. She said we had to take you with us to the Festival. We're just going to bathe and change. It's been a long day, we've been up since before dawn, but everything's ready now. Cook's pleased, and she jolly well should be. The roast swans look wonderful and the jellies are made into the most incredible shapes. You can't imagine!'

Fleabag slipped away, as Hal and the other kitchen boys swept Kern along in their excitement.

The cat trotted out of the servants' quarters and across the gardens towards the side entrance of the King's palace. The gravel pathways were already bitterly cold under his paws. There would be a hard frost tonight, and the daylight was fading fast.

He found Phelan and Gemma sitting in the library, which smelled of lavender and beeswax polish. The scent made Fleabag long for summer days. The cold weather was annoying him; he must be getting old.

The cat jumped up onto Gemma's lap and turned this way and that, purring as he trod his paws up and down on her knees and considered how he was going to make himself comfortable with the maximum inconvenience to Gemma.

Phelan laughed and scratched the cat's ears. 'How are you, my rat-chasing friend? Gemma says you are worried about our young visitor.'

Fleabag decided that the King's lap was bigger than Gemma's, and so probably more commodious.

He jumped across the gap and began to claw gently at Phelan's richly embroidered robes. The cat frowned as he looked up into Phelan's dark, golden-brown face. 'Indeed I am, and with good reason. I saw him with a blue crystal ball in the servants' quarters. He seemed to be peering into it very intently.'

Gemma leaned forward so she could speak quietly. She trusted all the palace servants, but if this lad was an enemy spy, then walls might have ears. 'Did he say anything into it?'

Fleabag shook his head. 'Not that I heard, but I think he was communicating somehow. He didn't look at all happy – in fact he looked quite miserable, and he was shivering the whole time he had it in his hand.'

Phelan stroked his black curly beard and frowned. 'Hmmm. What does the Ring Fire tell you, Gemma? Is he a danger or just a stray musician acting oddly?'

Gemma opened her hands and peered into the cup of her pink palms. Nothing glimmered. That didn't surprise her. The Ring Fire only burned when it was ready to. She was the Fire's servant, she never controlled it. But her skin *did* tingle.

'I don't think there's any immediate danger, but I will keep my hands open. Last time the wizards made a move I was completely taken in by Domnall and his smooth words! I was too wound up in my own miseries to see what was really happening. The Battle of Spider Island was all my fault and I won't let it happen again!'

Fleabag wrinkled his nose. 'I certainly hope not. I *told* you something was wrong at the time!' he smirked.

Phelan picked the cat up by the scruff of the neck

and peered at him. 'Listen, *Sir* Scrag-belly, if you speak to the Lady Fire Wielder in that tone of voice I'll have you skinned, boiled and fed to the field shrews for their Festival banquet!'

'Point taken, my Lord,' the cat replied meekly. Phelan was the only human he treated with the slightest glimmer of respect, for the King had once bested him in a fair fight – daggers to claws. 'But all the same,' the cat added, 'I feel in my whiskers that something is wrong.'

Gemma looked at her hands again with her head on one side as if she was listening. 'You know, I get the feeling that, for the moment at least, he isn't here for *us*... he's got some other purpose in mind.'

'Hmmm,' Fleabag screwed up his furry face. 'I'll keep an eye on him tonight. I'm *still* suspicious of anyone who could even contemplate using cat-gut for fiddle strings.'

3

The Fire Festival

As the sun went down, a trumpeter stood on the western balcony outside the Hall of Light. He raised a great brass horn to his lips and played a sad lament for the passing of the sun and the coming of the longest night.

The mournful sound was picked up and repeated by trumpeters across the city of Harflorum. Then there was silence. All the people were indoors. Everything was dark and still. No one ventured out into the market place, no one lit a candle or a lantern, fires and cooking stoves were extinguished, and everyone huddled under thick woollen blankets.

Kern tried to stop his teeth chattering as he stood amongst the kitchen staff and other servants at the back of the Hall of Light, waiting for total darkness. Then the great ceremony would begin. No one moved, no one breathed a word.

The Fire Wielder, dressed in a heavy cloak, did not move as she stood framed in the deepening dark of the eastern window, thrown open to the night winds.

Beside her, the King stood tall and equally still.

They did not flinch as an icy blast swept hail into their faces.

'What are they doing?' whispered Kern to Hal.

'Hush!' the older boy replied. 'You'll see.'

After about half an hour of seeming torture, when the last vestiges of light had long gone, the King threw back the hood of his cloak and sang in a rich, deep voice:

'There is no hope.
The great night has come,
the light has gone away.
There is no dawn.'

Then the Fire Wielder lifted up her arms and replied, singing:

'Fire Giver,
In our darkest hour,
give us light.
Breathe amongst us,
banish night.
Give us once more
the flame by which
we live and move,
and have our being.'

Then Kern could hardly believe his eyes, for a minute star appeared in the darkness. Everyone in the room gasped as the light swelled and deepened into a rich, warm, red-glow of living flame. They had all seen the full glory of the burning Fire many times before, but it never ceased to thrill them. Then the one light became two and Kern could see that each flame was born in the upraised palms of the Fire Wielder.

Kern bit his lip, for he knew enough magic to be able to tell that this was no trick, but real fire. Indeed, it was more than ordinary fire; it was *alive*.

His brother Domnall had taught him how to make fire. It was a beginner's trick, but that was nothing to the breathtaking beauty of this light. Despite himself, Kern was impressed. He would have to be very careful; this woman would be a formidable opponent.

The wizards had been wrong when they had told him the Fire Wielder knew no magic and was a naive inept. It seemed that she could *create*, and that was more than even his father or Sethan could do. They had only been good at destroying.

Suddenly he felt a sharp nudge in the ribs. 'The Light has come – pass it on.'

'What?'

Hal pushed a small lighted candle into Kern's fingers. 'The Light has come, pass it on!'

Kern suddenly realized he was expected to do something. A small boy on his left was looking up at him expectantly, holding a candle up to be lit.

'Oh, er – the Light has come, pass it on!' The boy grinned and turned to his neighbour, leaving Kern to stare in amazement at the little golden flame in his hands. This was just an ordinary candle flame, yet, yet there was something about it...

But he didn't have time to think for long. The windows in the Hall of Light had been shut against the winter gales, and everything was beginning to warm up, as candles were lit in every hand. High above, heavy crystal candelabras were hoisted into the huge glass lantern of the ceiling, making great mountains of swaying, glistening lights. Everywhere seemed suddenly to be awash with warmth and glowing colour and a heady scent of waxy sweetness.

Then the singing began. At first a few people began humming, and slowly others joined in, followed by fiddle and bodhran players near the front, swelling together into a joyful swaying tune. Then came the words. The people on the far side of the room seemed to be singing one line, with the people on Kern's side carolling an answer. Despite himself, Kern found that he too was humming, and even working out harmonies to the lilting melody.

Suddenly a blast of cold air made his flame flicker, as the main door to the hall was thrown open and the Fire Wielder moved through and down the stairs to the palace's main door below. Outside, the crowds that had gathered shouted, as the Fire Wielder and the King stepped outside and repeated their songs. The crowd cheered again as the Ring Fire flared up from the hands of the cloaked figure, spreading a golden glow across the city.

'Come on,' Hal urged. 'It's time for the feasting and dancing now. Aren't you playing music for us?'

Kern hesitated. 'I've never been to the Fire Festival before. I'd like to stay a bit longer and find out what happens next,' he said hopefully, craning his neck to see beyond the crowds gathered at the bottom of the stairs.

'Oh, I can tell you that,' Hal grinned. 'It's the same as you've just seen, but it happens over and over again. The Fire Wielder's bodyguard, the Princess Rowanne de Montiland, draws her sword and leads the Fire Wielder and the King through all the streets so they can hand the flame of the Ring Fire to anyone who comes with a candle. People take that flame home and light their fires and cooking stoves from it. Then everyone goes to their nearest hall or barn, then they dance and eat until they drop, sometime about dawn usually!'

'But why do they do it at all?' Kern asked. 'What's it for?'

'Well, there's a lot more to it than getting the kitchen fire going!' Hal laughed. 'But I'd have thought they'd have taught you that at least, where you come from! Look, I haven't got time to explain now, Cook needs us all to help carry food into the throne room. If you're not playing yet, can you lend us a hand?'

Late into the night, Kern sat propped against a pillar in the throne room, chewing on a chicken leg and swigging at a bottle of ginger cordial, watching the merrymaking. He felt full and happy. His music had been well received, he'd played jigs and reels until the dancers could dance no more. He'd been well paid and now he was eating the best food he had ever tasted in all his life.

Suddenly servants came into the room and extinguished all the lights. Everyone fell silent in the darkness. Kern sat bolt upright. Was there going to be more magic? But there were no icy winds this time, just a soft drumbeat that slowly became louder and louder. Soon Kern glimpsed a flickering light that seemed to move in time to the music. Then up on the stage, where he himself had been playing earlier, four figures dressed in black appeared, faintly outlined by the flaming torches they carried. The drum beat quickened and the two men and two women began to sway and move in time to the beat, swinging burning torches as they moved, reflecting warm gleams from heavy golden bangles around their wrists and arms. Kern was sure that the flowing black garments worn by the women would catch fire as they quickened their pace, swaying and dipping, swinging their arms this way and that. As the dancers moved, their flames left strange turquoise-coloured patterns that seemed to hang in the air like echoes of light.

Kern was mesmerized. He could not move; the ginger cordial spilled on the floor, but he did not notice, for the dancers were now throwing firebrands to each other, catching them as deftly as if they were ordinary juggler's clubs.

Then the drummers were joined by three more who played slightly different rhythms from each other, allowing the beats to twine and twist around each other. At the same time, all four of the fire dancers made their own pattern of flames, yet, with the music, they joined up with each other, tossing the firebrands into blazing patterns in the air.

With an abruptness that made Kern jump, the dancers stopped, with their burning torches held in a glowing star shape. After a few moments, the star pattern broke as one of the men moved into the middle and, collecting four of the torches, began to juggle, sending the brands high into the rafters.

The beat went on, faster and faster, and the juggling became more and more complex, yet the movements were as solemn and relentless as a heartbeat.

Then, with a final crash of the drums, the torches went out and there was silence in the pitch blackness.

Suddenly there was thunderous applause and candles were relit all around the room. The fire dancers were rewarded with gold and silver coins, and Kern even found himself throwing some of his hard-earned pence into the dancers' baskets as they came through the crowd.

'When it's dark like that, it makes you appreciate light and warmth, don't you think?'

Kern glanced around. Who had spoken?

'I'm down here, shrew-brain, unless you decide to be helpful and pick me up, so I can see better!'

Kern looked down and saw Fleabag getting his paws trodden on as people milled here and there to fetch food from the supper tables.

He picked the cat up. 'I suppose that's what the Festival is about, then? Is the Fire Wielder the wizard who makes light-magic in the darkness? Is that why it's held on the shortest day?'

'Sort of,' replied the cat. 'But it's nothing to do with magic or wizards. It re-enacts the Fire Giver giving us the Ring Fire, so we needn't be without help or afraid of evil any more. The Fire Wielder is just the servant who carries it for us. Grab me some fish from that plate, will you? Humans seem to get upset when I help myself.'

'Since when has that ever stopped you?' demanded a woman's deep voice from just behind them.

'I only need to help myself when you don't look after me properly!' sniffed the cat. 'But while someone fills up my plate for me, may I introduce my young friend Kern? Kern, this is the Princess Rowanne de Montiland, ruler of the royal city of Erbwenneth, and protector of the Fire Wielder's person.'

The Princess Rowanne de Montiland bowed her head briefly as she forked a large chunk of sea bass in aspic onto a plate. She handed it to Kern. 'Make sure you put it right under the table for him to eat, push it well back. He is *disgusting* when he eats. He slobbers, and the way he crunches bones makes my stomach turn!'

'But it's good for my teeth to chew!' protested Fleabag.

'Yes, my Lady,' Kern mumbled, and felt himself blushing as he bent down and pushed the food well out of sight.

'You played well earlier,' the Princess said kindly to Kern. 'You will be welcome in Erbwenneth.'

'Thank you, my Lady,' Kern muttered as the Princess strode away, her hand on the hilt of her gold sword as it flashed against her ceremonial flame-coloured silk tabard. Kern had been half blinded by her gold-plated breastplate, glittering with topaz and rubies set into the sign of the Ring Fire.

But, worse than that, the boy had felt a familiar and unwelcome blast of cold as he glimpsed the Princess' too-blue eyes. He bit his lip nervously.

'Oi!' said Fleabag, 'put me down, I'm famished, and if you grip me any harder, I'll snap!'

4

Kern's Message

So this was it! The moment he'd been dreading. He had found the person he was looking for.

When the Battle of Spider Island had been lost, Domnall had been sucked into his own spell and the Blue Magic had been reduced to ashes. The winds that had followed had scattered the ashes across the seas, where they could never be gathered again. But the wizards had looked into their scrying bowls and had seen that just one speck had been caught in the eye of a human, where it had stayed. The wizards could sense the speck was still alive, but who was the carrier? They knew that the right spells would rekindle the Blue Magic to its former power and strength, but the carrier had to be willing!

Kern had been sent to Harflorum to find someone whose eyes were 'too blue', the colour of Blue Magic, and to deliver him or her to Porthwain to be trained as a wizard. In no one else in the entire land would the Blue Magic be as potent or as pure as in the carrier of that one blue speck! The old Chancellor had failed to grasp the Kingdom, as had his sons Sethan and Domnall. The auguries had showed that if *this*

28

chance failed, then the wizards' power would dwindle and fade for ever.

Kern did not care about prophecies. All that mattered to him was that the wizards had promised that if he succeeded, he and his mother would be free to leave the University, to go wherever they wished. But if not then they would both remain as slaves of the wizards for ever. The wizards had not dared to go on this errand themselves, for the Ring Fire was strong in the hands of the Fire Wielder. She would know if any of them came near.

Even Kern could see he was the perfect choice for this errand. He nursed resentment against the Fire Wielder, but he was not a wizard so he would not be detected. Kern sensed he was a weak and easily expendable pawn in their deadly game. Blackmail and fear bound the boy to their slightest whim.

For his own part, Kern dared not contemplate failure. He could only think of the hope that success would bring. Yet he was very frightened. He hated working for the wizards, especially M'Kinnik. He knew their plans were evil, but what could he do against them? He would get this one job over, exact his own vengeance on the Fire Wielder, and then leave, never to think about the Blue Magic or the Ring Fire ever again. He would take his mother and together they would roam the world. He would play his music, and she would sing, and they would be free.

Suddenly a cheerful voice jerked him from his thoughts. 'Hello there, I enjoyed your playing.' It was Gemma, the maid who had been kind to him earlier. He rubbed his eyes sleepily. She was dressed in a formal court dress, made from red and gold silk. She must have had something very important to do in the Festival, although Kern hadn't noticed her in the Hall of Light.

'Thank you,' he yawned. 'Did you join the dancing?'

'No, I couldn't in this get-up,' Gemma smiled. 'But I was listening. If you'd like to stay around for a few weeks and play, you'd be welcome, and I'll bring Phelan along for a dance.'

'Thank you, I'd like that,' Kern nodded. Suddenly he remembered that he had work to do, and his quarry, the Princess Rowanne de Montiland, was already out of sight.

'Please don't think me rude, but I have to go; there is someone I must give an important message to.' Gingerly he began to move towards where he had last seen the Princess, talking with courtiers.

'Well, I'll see you around,' Gemma smiled. 'Goodnight.'

Kern turned and slipped amongst the crowds, but he could see no sign of the Princess. Terrified in case he had let her slip through his fingers, he darted along the grand corridors, peering this way and that, until he saw a few soldiers disappearing around a corner. They would know where the Princess' quarters were...

'Stop, please stop!' he called out, running as fast as he could behind them. Suddenly he tripped and tumbled onto the tiled walkway, rolling over. His violin twanged and cracked with a stomach-sickening noise, but Kern found himself crumpled in a heap at the feet of none other than the Princess Rowanne de Montiland herself.

Once more the boy shivered as he looked up at the Princess' too-blue eyes. The lady knight bent over and helped the boy up. 'I know why you're here,' she said quietly. 'You have a message for me.'

Kern sat miserably in a corner of the Princess' room, nursing the broken fragments of the violin across his knee. His eyes were stinging, but he told himself he was too old to cry – in public at least. He would scream and rage to his heart's content once he was alone.

Meanwhile, he was reciting the message of the wizards, word for word. He had learned it by heart. In fact he had been made to repeat it, before he was allowed to eat, every day for a month before he left Porthwain. It was engraved into his brain.

'My Lady, the Wizards of Porthwain greet you most humbly with the honour your most noble rank deserves. They have known and seen how, despite your noble personage's faithful service, the so-called Ring Fire has never recognized your true worth and great skill in the realms of magical power.

'It is the Wizards' intention, therefore, to rectify this great wrong to your noble self, and to invite you to the University at Porthwain as the guest of the most noble Chancellor and his wisest men and women for as long as it may please you. Here you may learn, at your leisure, the noble art of magic, for which the Wizards have not the slightest doubt that you were chosen and marked from the very moment of your conception.'

Kern sighed, but did not look up. The speech was over. He felt cold and drained, but he was almost free. Or he would be, if the Princess agreed to accompany him. That would be the difficult part.

Rowanne said nothing. She simply finished unstrapping her Ring Fire breastplate and laid it on the chair. Divested of her trappings, she was merely a dark-haired woman with a square face and determined eyes, for she was a lady knight by training as well as in title. Would she agree to go? Kern stole a sideways look. The candlelight reflected on the Ring Fire regalia, but through the window in the far wall daylight was beginning to stain the night sky with pale grey-blue streaks. Suddenly he felt an overwhelming sense of urgency. If only she would run out of the door with him now... this very second!

'Do you have proof?' she said at last, in a deep, slightly husky voice.

Kern put down the pieces of his violin and rummaged in his pocket until he drew out the blue velvet bag. Pulling the strings apart, he said: 'Would my Lady be so good as to open her hand?' And into her outstretched palm he gently tipped the blue crystal ball.

The Princess looked at the glassy depths and her eyes widened, although she said nothing. Kern knew she was meeting with M'Kinnik in thought.

Suddenly a firm knock sounded at the door. Kern jumped, but the Princess scarcely moved a muscle, except to close her hand around the ball. 'Come!' she called curtly.

The door opened and Fleabag entered, tail erect, golden earring gleaming. He was followed by a tall man with golden-brown skin and a thick black curly beard and hair. Behind him came a thin, freckle-faced girl: Gemma, the maid.

Kern reddened and felt embarrassed, although there was no reason why he shouldn't be there. He had a legitimate message, which was only between him and the Princess. He stepped back behind the door and tried to slip away, but the man shot out a strong arm and caught the boy around the wrist, firmly, but without hurting him. 'Wait there!' he ordered.

The Princess said nothing, but raised her chin defiantly.

'What's happening, Rowanne?' Gemma asked urgently. 'There is danger around. The Blue Magic is in the palace. I can see it plainly, I can feel my hands burning like they did on Spider Island. Something is happening, or is about to.'

Kern was amazed that the girl should speak to the Princess like an equal, but he said nothing.

'I suppose you know the boy's message? I expect the Ring Fire has told you already?' Rowanne raised a dark eyebrow and stared coldly at the visitors.

Gemma shook her head. 'Only that there is danger. And it is hovering around *you*, Rowanne. Ever since Spider Island, there has been something not quite right. But now it is coming alive. I'm sure the Ring Fire can help you…' and with that Gemma stepped forward and held out her hand, which cupped a warm, golden flame.

Kern gasped and jerked back. The tall man put his other hand reassuringly on the boy's shoulder. 'Don't worry, lad, Gemma is the Fire Wielder. Everything will be all right, she isn't really on fire, and she won't hurt the Princess. They are old friends.'

Kern stared wide-eyed at the man. How could this

friendly girl, only a little older than himself, be the evil woman he had sworn to kill? And how could he get the Princess away from her now? He slumped in the man's grip. All was lost. He was bound to be accused of wizardry. The only question now was, in which prison would he rot? Harflorum or Porthwain?

5

The Wizards' Challenge

But Kern did not have time to worry about his future.

An urgent hammering on the door made everyone jump. A breathless equerry entered and bowed to Gemma and Phelan. 'My Lady, your Highness... Forgive my intrusion, Princess, but news has come from the gates. A delegation has arrived from the University at Porthwain, and they are... forgive me for mentioning it,' he gasped, '... they are openly wearing insignia of the Brotherhood of Wizards!'

'Oh, I wish I'd had some sleep last night!' groaned Phelan, clutching his head.

'Your Highness,' the equerry bowed, 'may I suggest you get some sleep now, and we will receive the delegation at noon? I am sure they will want to rest as well.'

'Don't count on it,' Phelan sighed. 'They probably slept nearby last night and have only just woken up. They chose this moment because they knew we would be tired and not at our best. There is definitely something afoot.'

Kern looked up at his captor, open mouthed. *This*

was the King? Of course, the King's name was Phelan, and he had sung beautifully last night. Gemma had said her friend Phelan was a wonderful singer. Why hadn't he been more careful when making friends at the palace? He should have been more aware that things had been too easy. They probably had been warned of his presence by this Ring Fire of theirs and he had walked straight into a trap. Kern hated himself for being so stupid.

Gemma scooped up Fleabag and turned to the equerry. 'Give the Princess a guard; she may be in danger. And take the boy Kern to a room where he can be comfortable, but carefully watched. We will receive the delegation at noon, as you suggest. Feed our guests from Porthwain and provide them with hot baths and comfortable guest suites. With any luck they will be tired, and they might be tempted to sleep rather than to get up to mischief.'

'I wouldn't bet on it,' muttered Fleabag.

When they were outside the door, the cat whispered, 'Put me down, Gemma. I want to keep an eye on things here.'

Gemma scratched her furry friend behind his ear as she wished him happy hunting. As she straightened, she noticed that Kern looked very dejected as he was led away by a guard.

She ran down the corridor to catch him up. 'Don't worry. You aren't in trouble, we're just a bit concerned at the moment. I'm certain you aren't the real danger. You can go for a walk in the grounds or play your violin if you like. You aren't in prison. I will come and see you later; I think we need to talk.'

Kern glowered at her. He despised himself for

liking her earlier, so now he hated her. She must be trying to lull him into a false sense of security, so he'd betray the wizards without realizing it. He scowled and hung his head, saying nothing.

Gemma tried again. 'I'll have your violin sent to you, if you like. Where did you leave it?'

'Smashed, in the Princess' room. Doesn't matter though,' he grunted.

Gemma turned to the guard. 'Make sure a very good violin is provided for this boy. He is my personal guest.'

And with that she turned and followed Phelan out into the garden that separated the royal private chambers from the main body of the palace.

The icy chill of the night was beginning to lift as the early morning air warmed a little in the dawn.

'I am going to my room to consult the Ring Fire. You get some sleep, and call me before you meet the delegation. We can talk then.'

At half-past eleven, the King knocked on the Fire Wielder's door and waited. There was no reply. He knocked again, and at last a sleepy voice called, 'Come in.'

Gemma looked as if she had slept in a heap. Her clothes were dishevelled and her hair was tousled. She groaned as she glanced at the clock. 'Oh no! I came and sat down, meaning to look into the Ring Fire, and I must have fallen asleep straight away. This is terrible.'

'Never mind,' the King answered. 'Straighten yourself up a bit, and come with me to meet the wizards. When we know what they are here for, you can make time to do things properly.'

'We had better ask Rowanne to be there.' Gemma looked worried. 'If she is in some kind of danger from the wizards, we might be able to see what it is. If we hide her from them, the danger may remain hidden too.'

'I'd be glad of her presence for other reasons, I must admit,' Phelan added. 'If the wizards' visit has any military implications, I want Rowanne to be the first to know. We are going to need all the help we can get.'

'Shall we ask the boy, Kern, to be there?'

'No.' Phelan shook his head. 'Did you see his face? He was terrified when he heard the wizards were coming. He's involved, but not willingly, I'd wager. He knows something, but showing him to the wizards now won't help anyone.'

Meanwhile, the Princess Rowanne de Montiland had not slept. The few hours she had been alone she had peered unceasingly into the blue crystal ball that Kern had put into her hand. During that whole time, she had not uttered a word, nor had she moved a muscle. But when she got up to answer the summons to audience, her eyes were even bluer than before.

The wizards were already seated in the throne room when the King and the Royal Fire Wielder entered. The Princess followed behind, with Fleabag hiding beneath the copious sweeping folds of her long woollen cloak. He knew the wizards would be angered by his presence – they hated cats, especially black ones – and he did not feel like being fried by Blue Magic this early in the morning. Anyway, he wanted to keep within a claw's scratch of his old arch-enemy, Rowanne, just in case...

Chancellor M'Kinnik was a fat, sour-faced man in his early sixties. On his right and left were his two Vice Chancellors, one a tall, beautiful woman of about middle age, very black-skinned and obviously from the far south of the Kingdom, and the other, an elderly, almost skeletal old man with a bald head. All were dressed in richly embroidered blue silk robes, and heavy indigo-dyed fur cloaks.

None of them rose as the royal party entered; they just stared rudely at Gemma as she took her place, making her feel decidedly uncomfortable. The King bowed formally to his guests and started to greet them cordially with a speech of welcome.

M'Kinnik was obviously not listening, and after a sentence or two, he suddenly stood and interrupted the King.

'Look, I'm not interested in pleasantries.' He slapped the table with the flat of his hand. 'We're here to issue the Great Challenge. Three trials, and whoever wins takes the crown *and* the Ring Fire. Once and for all. No more silly petty battles, no more arguments. A fair fight according to the rules. Tests of strength, wisdom and magic.'

Phelan stood amazed with his mouth open, staring in disbelief, not only at the Chancellor's rudeness, but at the Challenge itself.

The Chancellor then nodded to the beautiful woman, who stood and unrolled a scroll. 'According to the law of the land, laid down by the Fire Giver himself, if a ruler or Fire Wielder is suspected unfit to rule, then three trials may be set in the Great

Challenge. Whoever performs the trials without defeat is then undisputed monarch for ever.'

Phelan and Gemma looked at each other. It was by this Law of Challenge that Rowanne had become the Princess of Erbwenneth. There was no disputing the fact that the wizards had every right to do this. The King was sweating as he clenched and unclenched his hands. Gemma turned deathly pale and shivered.

Suddenly Rowanne leaned forward. Her face was flushed, and her eyes sparkled with excitement. 'Good!' she whispered hoarsely. 'Now's our chance! Accept, Gemma, and we can be rid of the wizards for ever!'

Phelan stared at the Princess in disbelief. 'You're serious, aren't you?'

Rowanne sat absolutely straight in her chair. 'Perfectly. And why not? We have the Ring Fire, and surely that is more powerful than the Blue Magic. What have we to fear?'

M'Kinnik gave a small signal to his companions. 'We did not come here to listen to you squabbling amongst yourselves. You have until sunset tonight. If the Challenge isn't accepted, then we have no choice but to declare war on Harflorum. Then any deaths will be on your heads. It will not be our fault; you will have had the choice to take the peaceful and honourable way out! Good day.' And with that he swept his great fur cloak around him and walked out of the room, without even waiting to be dismissed or bowing to the King and the Fire Wielder. Fleabag hissed as the throneroom doors were shut behind the backs of the retreating wizards.

'Well!' declared Fleabag, crawling out from under

Rowanne's cloak and jumping onto the table. 'By my whiskers, I declare that of all the blackmailing rats I have ever seen, they take the prize!' The cat jumped up onto the polished oak table and began to pace up and down. 'How disgusting, how dishonourable, how, how...'

'How much are your claws scratching the wood?' Gemma chided, lifting the cat onto her lap. His hackles were raised and his great lantern eyes glowed as if they were live coals in his scraggy face. 'Let me go after them, Gemma! I'll show them, I'll scratch their nasty blue eyes and pee on their spell books, I'll...'

'You'll do nothing of the sort,' Gemma said firmly. 'In all seriousness, what do you think, Phelan?'

The King leaned back in his chair and sighed. 'Well, legally, they have every right to do this. The fact that they *believe* we are bad rulers is enough for them to issue the Challenge. They don't need permission or a provable case. The proof will be in their success.'

'Or failure,' Fleabag added sourly.

Gemma looked at her old friend Rowanne. 'Why do you think it's such a good idea?'

'Well, as I said, it's obvious. The Ring Fire is so much stronger than the Blue Magic and it cannot be won or taken anyway. It is the gift of the Fire Giver, so I don't see that a Challenge can be a problem. Let us accept, prove our point, then settle down to peaceful lives, knowing the question of who should be King and Fire Wielder is settled for ever. I, for one, have a great deal to do at Erbwenneth, and I would like to get on with it.'

'Why are you convinced it will be so easy, Rowanne? We almost failed twice before.' Gemma wished she could have Rowanne's courage when danger threatened. Her friend was a trained warrior, but, for her part, Gemma still felt more at home in the kitchen than handling affairs of State or working with the Ring Fire in a real crisis.

Rowanne leaned across the table. 'Think about it. What happened to the Blue Magic when Domnall fell into his own spell?'

'Everything turned to blue ash,' Phelan replied, looking perplexed.

'Exactly!' Rowanne replied enthusiastically. 'And the ash?'

'It blew away across the sea,' Gemma replied.

'So the Blue Magic must be very weak. Even a wizard could not collect up all the specks of dust from everywhere, unless their powers were very great, and they can't be...'

'Because the Blue Magic blew away, so their power is weakened. I see,' Phelan said thoughtfully.

Gemma said nothing, but stared hard at the palms of her hands. 'The Ring Fire looks rather odd today, but maybe it's because I'm tired. I wish they would give us more time. How real would their threat of war be?' She looked across at Rowanne.

The Princess was trying hard to contain her excitement at the possibility of getting to Porthwain so easily. Secretly, she could not wait to take up the wizards' offer of going to the University. 'Give me leave to go, Gemma, and I will asses the situation. We could visit Porthwain and talk with their advisors about the Challenge, without saying yes or no. Then, once there, I could find out all sorts of things about their strategic strength.'

Phelan and Gemma exchanged glances. 'I'm not happy about you going, Rowanne,' Gemma said. 'I still feel there is a great danger very close to you.'

The Princess looked offended. She pursed her lips and scowled. 'I am a knight of many years' experience. I think I know how to look after myself. I am certain I can stall the decision for a few weeks at least. It's time we're buying, and knowledge. If we rush a decision we'll make a mistake that we'll regret deeply for a very long time to come.' She squeezed the little crystal ball as she spoke, and wondered why the stone remained so cold in her hand. But she did not look; she did not want the others to see it.

Gemma nodded and rose to her feet. 'I will consult the Ring Fire.'

The King beckoned to his equerry. 'Summon my ministers. I need an urgent meeting in half an hour.'

Fleabag jumped down from the table onto the floor. 'And I will nose around the stables and see whether the wizards have any intelligent horses with them. Horses tend to know everything that's worth knowing. I'll see what I can find out.'

'We will meet here just before sunset then,' Phelan said.

In an upstairs room, Kern cowered well away from the window. He knew M'Kinnik was mind-searching for him, but the Princess had the crystal ball. Kern did not strictly need the stone. He had only to open his mind. The ball simply helped him to focus. But now he did not want to be found.

He had not even looked at the new violin he had

43

been given. Miserably he fingered the fragments of his old one that a servant had salvaged for him. He dabbled a brush into a pot of wood glue and plotted revenge.

6

The 'Sending'

'The wizards conduct a fair fight? By my paws and whiskers, that'll be the day!' Fleabag grumbled as he sat on the window sill of Gemma's room. 'Anyway, I don't know how we can answer their Challenge by sunset. There are thick clouds everywhere, and it's beginning to snow. No one can see the sun setting at all.' He twitched his tail irritably.

'It'd be about as fair a fight as I would expect from *you*,' Gemma retorted.

Fleabag sniffed. 'My dear wife Tabitha says I am the most honourable mouser she knows. I *always* wait until the dear creatures have eaten before I pounce. Even a condemned rodent is entitled to its last meal, I always say!'

'Rubbish!' Gemma snorted. 'What you mean is you wait until the poor things are nice and fat before you gobble them up!'

'Well, if the kitchen staff fed me properly, I wouldn't need to hunt to keep a fur coat over my poor old bones!' he sighed. 'I really am wearing away to nothing; Tabitha says so.'

Gemma stretched out an arm and scooped her old

friend onto her lap. 'You're fed well enough, you old rascal. You should be living in luxurious retirement and leaving your kittens and grand-kittens to keep the mouse population down.'

Fleabag growled his deep, rolling purr and turned his barrel-like tummy upwards, demanding to be stroked. 'But the long and the short of it is, I don't trust those wizards further than the length of a shrew's tail. That fiddle player Kern is involved, but he doesn't *smell* bad. Rowanne is in danger, and something in her pocket *does* smell decidedly bad!'

'What do you mean, "in her pocket"?'

'Dunno.' The cat gave a wild squirm and jumped up to the window sill again. 'It just does.'

Phelan looked at the darkening skies. 'It must be nearly sunset. What is our decision?'

Gemma opened her hands and looked at the tiny glow of Ring Fire that nestled in her palms. 'Something *is* wrong. Fleabag got no sense out of the wizards' horses whatsoever. It could be that they are all under a spell of stupidity, or they are particularly "dumb beasts". Either way, he found out nothing from them.'

'They were really strange!' Fleabag added. 'They just looked straight through me as if I didn't exist. They really gave me the shivers, I can tell you!'

'Anyway,' Gemma continued, 'I get the feeling that it would be a good idea to go to Porthwain. I'm certain that this Challenge idea is a trap, but I do feel that the Ring Fire wants us to go. Perhaps to put paid to the wizards once and for all.'

'I think the same,' Phelan nodded. 'But my ministers have come up with an interesting twist to the

Challenge. Apparently, by law, if we accept, we also have the right to set three trials of our own. This means that even if we fail the wizards' trials, if they fail ours as well, they cannot claim the crown or any position or title anywhere. The whole thing will be thrown completely open, for they will be deemed to be unfit challengers.'

Gemma smiled. 'That's good. So we accept Rowanne's plan that we should send an emissary to Porthwain. We will say we wish to discuss the Challenge, but without accepting or rejecting it. This will give us time to try to understand what is happening and how the Ring Fire wants us to handle it.'

'Agreed,' Phelan said. 'What do you say, Fleabag?'

The cat looked down from his perch. 'I agree too. But whom should we send?'

'Rowanne wants to go, but I'm sure it's too dangerous for her,' Gemma said thoughtfully. 'She has never really understood why the Blue Magic can't be fought with swords and shields.'

Phelan stroked his beard and wrinkled his forehead. 'Neither you nor I can go until the twelve days of the Fire Festival are over. There's so much to do...'

'Forget the Fire Festival,' Fleabag interrupted urgently, peering out of the window. 'Look down there in the distance, beyond the gates... It's Rowanne, I'd recognize the way she sits on a horse anywhere. And who's on that second horse, behind her?'

Gemma gasped. 'By the shape of that peculiar basket across his back, I'd say it must be Kern, the fiddle player!'

Gemma and Phelan dashed from the room, followed hotly by Fleabag, running as fast as his three legs allowed.

Phelan called to a guard to send out soldiers to stop the travellers. But as they reached the great doors, the Captain of the Guard met them, quite out of breath. 'We cannot stop them, your Highness; all the horses have been lamed and the palace gates have been jammed shut, though we cannot work out how.'

Phelan and Gemma exchanged glances. 'The wizards! Where are they?'

The Captain shook his head and shrugged. 'They have gone too, Sire. In fact, it's very odd. They left so suddenly, no one saw them go. There weren't even tracks in the snow. In fact, no one saw them arrive either. They were just here, then they were gone!'

Gemma felt herself go white. 'It was all a "sending".'

'A what?' asked Phelan, bemused.

'It was a sending – an illusion. The wizards weren't really here at all. They sent images of themselves. That was how they managed to turn up just at the most awkward time possible. They must have smuggled something into the palace by which they could watch us, and scry our movements.'

'That's probably what stank in Rowanne's pocket!' Fleabag added. 'I thought it was rather worse than dog-breath. Humph!'

'But it would also explain why you could get no sense from their horses. They weren't really there either. They just sent us illusions of horses, so we wouldn't suspect anything until it was all too late! I wonder if that *was* Kern riding with Rowanne?'

Gemma beckoned to a maid standing nearby. 'Go up to the guest quarters where the boy musician was staying, and bring him to me.'

'Oh, I can tell you now, your Ladyship,' the girl curtseyed. 'He's gone. The Princess Rowanne came and demanded he went with her, urgent-like, about half an hour ago. I had to fetch food and wine for the journey. They seemed in a terrible hurry, and the boy was kicking up a fuss. But the Princess showed him something, and he quietened down, all of a sudden. After that, he went, meek as a lamb.'

'Did you see what she showed the boy? Quick, it's important,' Phelan demanded.

'No, your Highness. I was packing saddlebags on the other side of the room. But whatever it was, it was definitely a nasty blue colour. I glimpsed that for sure.'

Gemma bit her lip and frowned. 'Is there anything else you can remember, anything at all?'

'No, your Ladyship,' the girl replied, 'except… except one thing. I think what he was screaming about was his fiddle. The Princess wouldn't let him take it. There was a really posh violin in there, but that wasn't what he was fussing about. He wanted the old broken one. He left it behind when the Princess calmed him down, though.'

'What happened to it? Can you remember?' Gemma asked urgently.

The girl blushed. 'Begging your pardon, Ma'am, and I hope I didn't do nothing wrong, but I took it upstairs for my little brother. It's only a bit broke, and my brother's always wanted a fiddle.'

Gemma sighed with relief. 'Good. Fetch it, and

you will be given the other violin for your brother.'

The girl ran, and Phelan looked puzzled. 'Why is an old broken fiddle so important?'

'It's just that Kern loved it. It was probably the only thing he had in the world. Perhaps someone he cared about gave it to him. Who knows? It obviously meant more to him than just something to play to earn money. He's a very sad boy. If we can give him back a bit of happiness then that's what we must do.

'But first things first: we must get these gates open.'

And with that, she strode to the main entrance. Without hesitating she circled the locks on the huge iron gate-catches with the sign of the Ring Fire, and one by one they snapped apart. Similarly, the horses responded to her touch. 'There was nothing wrong with them,' she told the amazed stablehand. 'They were spellbound, that's all.'

'What do we do now?' asked Phelan. 'It's too dark and cold to go after them tonight.'

Gemma looked up at the swirling snow falling against the bitter blackness. 'But they won't get far either, even with the Blue Magic to help them. The boy has none, and we don't know how much Rowanne carries. I suspect not much. Tonight, we get some sleep, and at first light we set off after them.'

7

In Pursuit

Kern said nothing as he rode, day after miserable day, next to the Princess. The snow had soon turned to rain, and the countryside was grey and muddy. High above in the cold, dark skies crows circled endlessly, calling their lonely cries into the wind.

The boy hung his head, pulled his thick cloak tightly around him and kept pace. He felt a deep sense of foreboding and loneliness. He tried to think about how delighted he had been when the Princess had told him he was to accompany her to Porthwain. He told himself he would surely get his freedom when he delivered her to the Chancellor. He had been frightened that the Fire Wielder and the King would dissuade her from going, but it had all been so easy!

But these thoughts did little to lift his mood. Kern was angry. The Princess had not allowed him to stop even for a few seconds to pick up his violin. And he had almost had it mended, too! He would never forgive her for that. He would return to get his vengeance on Gemma and the King some other time. He ground his teeth and clenched the horse's reins in his icy hands. At least he would see his mother soon, and they would both be free from the wizards' service for ever. Moreover, things could be worse. He had arrived at Harflorum hungry and on foot. Now he was returning on a horse, well fed, and with good clothes on his back.

For her part, the Princess wanted Kern alive and well when they reached Porthwain. The boy's message had been a strange one. If the invitation to spend time at the University was genuine, then it was important that the wizards' emissary must appear to have been honoured and well cared for. If, on the other hand, she was being made a fool of, she would slit Kern's throat. She had no qualms about that.

Rowanne had so many reasons for making this journey, even she was not sure which one was most important to her.

On the one hand, she was fairly sure that the boy was some sort of bait, and if anyone was going to walk into a trap it must be herself and not Gemma or Phelan, for in her heart she was still loyal to the King and the Fire Wielder. She cared very much about them both. Gemma wasn't much more than a child, and she had been through enough terrible battles. Phelan was needed to concentrate on being the King and attending to matters of State. There was much to be done to maintain justice in the land. Rowanne felt it was *her* turn to fight a battle to protect the Ring Fire – by whatever means possible. If she could learn some of the secrets of the Blue Magic, she could tell Gemma and use her knowledge to help the Ring Fire win this Challenge and settle matters in the land, once and for all.

She could not understand why Phelan and Gemma were so scared of the Challenge anyway. If the Ring Fire was on their side, who could be against them? She had left Harflorum suddenly, because she was convinced that the time had come to be decisive. She wasn't going to wait to be mocked by the wizards or told to be patient by Gemma. *She* would accept the Challenge on everyone's behalf, and the more of the Blue Magic's secrets she knew to help her win, the better it would be for the Ring Fire!

And, as the wizards' message had said, it was also true that she had always felt passed over by the Ring Fire. Whenever she had tried to use her sword and her battle skills to defend what she knew to be true, she was always told 'this isn't that sort of battle'. What did Gemma know? This was Rowanne's big chance to prove her own worth.

The journey took ten days, for the roads were slushy and difficult. Kern was exhausted and often dozed in the saddle. But Rowanne never seemed to sleep. At night, when they stopped at an inn or a lodging house, she would eat her meal and find a quiet corner. There she would unwrap the blue crystal and stare into it until dawn, unspeaking and unmoving as the pale blue glow bathed her face and hands. Kern closed his mind tightly and turned away, with bed covers over his head. He did not want to know... he did *not* want to know...!

Rowanne had been to Porthwain before, and had been drugged and charmed into a deep sleep by the old Chancellor. He had used ruthless spells to take her mind from her body so she would betray the

Ring Fire. She had almost died. Rowanne's ambition to be taken seriously as a Champion of the Ring Fire was so great she pushed all those terrible memories aside. She did not realize that her education in the Blue Magic was already well under way, and that, as she stared into the crystal ball, the tiny speck of blue that had caught in her eye on Spider Island had begun to grow and spread within her like fine tendrils of mould. Rowanne's skin was already taking on a strange blue tinge, and her eyes glowed with an unearthly ice-blue stare. By the time she had arrived, the Princess Rowanne de Montiland was already nearly an arch wizard.

The delegation of soldiers, dressed in ceremonial dark- and light-blue uniforms, that greeted her at the gates of the town and escorted her to the university, did not surprise her. She had foreseen it.

Back at Harflorum, delay after delay prevented Gemma, Fleabag and Phelan from pursuing Rowanne. Each problem was petty and annoying and had the mark of the wizards' work. But the delays cost three days.

Phelan and Gemma delegated their Fire Festival duties, and Fleabag spent extra time with Tabitha and the kittens. Phelan would only accept a bodyguard of three men and his sergeant at arms. The more travellers there were, the more equipment and food would be needed. Speed was of the essence. The Prime Minister complained bitterly, and Rowanne's faithful squire Aidan begged to come along, but he was refused as well. Even Fleabag did not try to smuggle any of his kittens into a saddlebag this time.

At dawn on the fourth day, six swift horses were saddled and four more were loaded with essentials for the journey. Gemma let the Ring Fire burn for a few moments in her hands to cheer them all up, then she swung into the saddle and dug her heels into her horse's flanks. The great gates of Harflorum swung wide, and the travellers set off.

Persistent rain kept their roads clear, but made everyone feel miserable. Day after day, they rode as hard as they could without exhausting the horses. They stopped at farms and inns, and often heard that Rowanne and Kern had been that way only a few days earlier.

Every evening, when they had found lodging, Gemma watched the Ring Fire in her hands, with Fleabag and Phelan either side, caught in the beauty of its glow for an hour or more. It gave them the heart to keep going.

'Can you tell what Rowanne is doing?' Phelan asked one night as they neared Porthwain. 'Are we too late?'

Gemma shook her head and folded her hands so the fire was enclosed. 'No, the Ring Fire's not like the Blue Magic. I can't see what *I* think I need to see. Only what it wants to show me. Most of the time I don't see anything, but I can usually tell whether something is right or wrong. I have been trying to surround Rowanne with the glow of the Fire, but it keeps slipping away, for some reason. It won't stick. It works for Kern, though. He's safe, I'm sure, but I'm very worried about Rowanne.'

Phelan tugged at his beard and frowned. 'Do you remember when she was in that terrible trance-like sleep after she went to Porthwain the first time? When you tried to put the Ring Fire on her to waken her, it kept slipping away then as well?'

'Yes I do,' Gemma sighed. 'And that is what is worrying me. It's all too similar. But this time I don't think they want to take her mind from her. The wizards have a different plan. She seemed awfully keen to go when she heard about the Challenge. I think the best thing we can do is to get to Porthwain as quickly as possible, before too much damage is done.'

Fleabag jumped up onto Gemma's lap and began to scratch himself hard, spraying a few fleas onto his friend's clothes.

'Ugh, you're *disgusting!*' she groaned, and tried to put him down.

'Well, if you don't want to hear what I've got to say, I shall go and tell it to the mice behind the skirting board.' Fleabag bristled his fur and began to stalk away on his three legs, head held high and whiskers splayed.

Phelan scooped the cat up and peered into his eyes. 'Well, you *are* disgusting… But you do have your uses. What is it that you remember?'

'Rowanne said something about a message…'

'I remember that too. Did you find out what it was?' Phelan asked.

The cat shook his head. 'No, but she did say that Kern had delivered it.'

'So he *was* a spy from the wizards?' Phelan gasped.

'Not a willing one,' Gemma replied. 'He was terrified when he heard that the wizards had arrived. But after the Fire Festival, in the throne room, I was talking to Kern and he scurried off, saying he had to deliver a message.'

'There was the awful smell that hung around Rowanne's pocket. I think Kern must have given her something from the wizards,' Fleabag added.

'Something that they could then use to create their sending with!' Gemma opened her hand and looked into the tiny speck of Ring Fire that burned there. 'I am certain it *is* right for us to go to Porthwain, but we will have to be very careful.'

Fleabag leaped from Phelan's lap onto the hearth rug and curled up. 'And to be prepared for this great adventure, I am going to get some beauty sleep. I feel in my whiskers that this is going to be a bit like swimming in a bowl of goldfish who are all twenty times my size, and all bent on revenge.'

'But,' Gemma added thoughtfully, 'who knows? Just as there are probably little bits of Blue Magic in our own palace at Harflorum, we might find the Ring Fire burning somewhere in the University. I can't imagine that there can be anywhere within this world that is entirely without hope.'

Fleabag grunted through his thick tangled fur, 'I'm not sure about that. I've munched a fair few goldfish in my time.' And he went to sleep.

8

Rowanne the Wizard

Kern wasn't particularly surprised to find himself being ignored in Porthwain. He didn't exactly expect the blue carpet rolled out for *his* arrival.

But what upset him deeply, was that his mother was missing. The kitchen staff she usually worked with said that she had disappeared soon after he had left. He went to the attic room they used to share, and found all their things were gone. The room was occupied by two foul-mouthed and extremely smelly stable hands who neither knew nor cared about Kern or his mother.

Kern tried to see M'Kinnik to ask if he knew anything, for his mother *was* a wife of the old Chancellor even though she had always been badly treated. He also wanted to claim his long-promised freedom.

But however often he called on the Chancellor's secretary's office door, he was always told that his Holiness was out or busy, or to come back next week, or month, or year.

Finally, he was given a huge pile of papers to fill in (in triplicate) about his mother and himself. He was told that once that information was on file, procedures for tracing his mother's whereabouts and considering his application for release from the University's service could be put into motion.

Kern didn't believe any of it, but he took the papers up to the loft above the barn where he now slept.

But, as he crossed the stableyard, he saw a strange sight – one he had never quite expected to see in Porthwain. Ten horses were being led across the cobbles. They were fine animals, though very tired and sweaty. There was nothing unusual in that, but what did catch his eye was the Ring Fire symbol, embroidered in gold and red silk on the saddlecloths.

Letting go of his papers – which landed in the nearest horse-trough – Kern ran back inside and crept along a top corridor until he came to the servants' entrance to the Great Hall.

There, in full view, were Gemma the Fire Wielder and King Phelan, being received most politely by M'Kinnik, the Chancellor of All Wizards. And sitting smugly at their feet was Fleabag, the irrepressible three-legged talking cat!

Fleabag spotted Kern as well. Knowing that he created a stir everywhere he went in Porthwain, he got up on his three legs and calmly strolled across the hall to where Kern peered around the doorway. 'Excuse me,' the cat called back to his friends. 'I've found a rather fascinating mouse.'

The Chancellor blanched at the sound of the cat's voice, for all the wizards had a particular terror of Fleabag. An old prophecy had warned that Porthwain's downfall would be caused by a Fire Maiden and a black cat. Even after the Battle of

Porthwain when Gemma and Fleabag had defeated the old Chancellor, everyone still held a deep-seated conviction that all black cats were evil, though the city was still standing and the Blue Magic was still alive.

Fleabag didn't care. He slunk around the door-jamb. 'Hello,' he mewed. Before Kern could move, Fleabag had leaped into the boy's arms and was licking his face like a long-lost friend.

'Ugh!' Kern tried to push him away. But the cat was not going to allow himself to be put down just yet.

'Come to our room after dinner,' he whispered, 'and I guarantee you will have a very pleasant surprise.' Then he jumped down and stalked back into the reception room where polite speeches of welcome were being made. There he sat down in the very middle of the room, burped extremely loudly, and began to wash.

The wizards glanced nervously at one another, but the Chancellor just smirked and complimented his visitors on having such an entertaining pet.

Phelan bowed and requested leave for them all to go to their rooms, as they, and their *friend* the cat, were very tired.

Upstairs Phelan and Gemma unpacked and then met in the small circular study that had been assigned to them. Fleabag had already taken command of the hearthrug in front of the fire. He did not look happy. 'Isn't it strange how a suite of rooms was ready for us? This fire has been lit all morning, I'd say.'

'They were expecting us,' Gemma agreed.

'I'm certain of it,' Phelan replied. 'But they were talking as if the Challenge had been accepted and was due to start in a few days' time. How can that be?'

'It must be Rowanne. What on earth has she done?' Gemma groaned.

'I expect we will find out soon,' Fleabag replied. 'But the good news is that I've found Kern. I've told him to come up and see us after dinner.'

'And did he say he'd come?' Phelan asked.

'Well,' the cat replied, 'he looked sort of worried, but I think he will.'

Just then, a servant knocked on the door. 'I have a humble request from the Princess Rowanne de Montiland, wizard of this University, if it please you, to meet her in the library when you have refreshed yourselves.'

Phelan thanked the girl and shut the door carefully behind her. *'Wizard of this University?'*

Gemma had her right hand resting on the table in front of her and was staring at the Ring Fire burning there. 'Yes. Things are getting very dangerous indeed.'

An hour later, Phelan, Fleabag and Gemma crossed the piazza where they had once rescued Rowanne from the burning hall after defeating the old Chancellor. Everything was rebuilt now, and there was no sign of fire on the milky white stone of the wide columned entryway.

On the other side of the square was an equally grand building housing the library. Servants ushered the visitors into the main room, a long cool gallery, lit by many windows all along the walls. The books were arranged in wide bays, with ancient gold script describing the contents of each section. Every bay was three or four metres high, and filled, floor to ceiling, with books, all leather-bound and very old. Strange sliding ladders hung from rails at the top of each bookcase, so the volumes on the uppermost shelves could be reached.

As the visitors stared up at the ceiling they saw that above the ground floor there were two more galleried floors, similarly filled with books, all the way up to a finely vaulted ceiling high above them.

Just then Rowanne's familiar voice called down cheerfully from above the balustrade around the top floor. 'Oh good, you're here at last! I knew you couldn't be far away. Just a moment, I'll be down!' And with that she disappeared.

Gemma and the others felt a moment's relief to be greeted so warmly, but their hearts sank, and their skin went quite cold when they saw their friend *floating* down the ornate spiral staircase, one hand resting lightly on the gently curving banister. Her feet hovered just above the steps as the uncanny silence of her motion was broken only by the light swishing of her clothing brushing the wrought iron-work at the side.

Rowanne was dressed in fine robes of dark and light blue, with her long black hair brushed loosely over her shoulders. She looked very beautiful, although her skin and eyes were quite blue, and even her lips were purple.

Fleabag surveyed her for a moment and put his head on one side. 'You couldn't possibly want me for a fur collar now, Rowanne. I'm entirely the wrong colour – I wouldn't match your skin!'

The Princess stooped down to pick him up and laughed as she rubbed him under the chin. '*Dear*

Fleabag, you are always so amusing. What a pleasure to see you all here. Now, we have some talking to do.' And she put the cat down.

He immediately began to wash and scratch all over, as if he had been touched by something disgusting. 'Ugh, I smell of poodles now!' he muttered.

But Rowanne ignored him, and gestured to a small reading table in a corner by a window.

'I am so pleased you could come. The Challenge is fixed for three days hence. But I expect you are all prepared and raring to go, aren't you?'

Gemma suddenly stood and leaned across the table. 'Rowanne. Snap out of it! What *are* you blabbering on about? You know we agreed not to accept the Challenge. The plan was to stall and play for time. You aren't even supposed to *be* here! It was quite wrong of you to accept the Challenge on our behalf. It can't hold as an acceptance. You had no authority.'

Rowanne shook her head and smiled. 'But we're committed. What's the harm? The Ring Fire cannot possibly fail, especially with me on its side.'

Phelan and Gemma exchanged glances. There was a moment's silence, then, 'What do you mean, exactly?' Gemma ventured.

Rowanne grinned and winked. 'I've learned loads of their secrets. They've been teaching me to become a wizard.'

'We did notice,' Fleabag muttered. 'It sort of shows, you know.'

'Well,' Rowanne grinned. 'The joke is, that although I've been here working for the Ring Fire, *they* think I'm working for them, and that I'm going to be a good wizard, and a true member of the University. I've been working really hard during the last few days, and I've qualified already.'

'But it must take years, surely!' Phelan protested.

'Normally, yes,' Rowanne replied. 'But you remember that speck I caught in my eye after the Battle of Spider Island? Apparently it was a tiny bit of Blue Magic ash, and because it's *inside* me it works really fast. So I've read the whole library and done all the practical work in less than a week!'

Gemma went pale. So that speck of dust had been Blue Magic. She stared at her old friend in horror: 'The *whole* library?'

'Yes, it's dead easy, look.' Ignoring the ladders, she floated up to the top of one of the bays, and picked out a book at random. 'All I have to do is hold the book to my head for a few seconds, and I can read and memorize the lot. Look,' she passed the book over to Phelan, 'test me.'

Phelan looked at the book. '*The Logik of Transformation Described and Discussed*, by Professor Cumthidymus.'

'Go on,' Rowanne urged. 'Open it, any page, any line…'

Phelan opened the book. It crackled as the dry leather moved. 'Er, tell me what's on page 276, third line up from the bottom.'

Rowanne laughed, 'Oh yes, that's the very witty part where he proposes that transformation of one object into another is perfectly possible, because in essence, nothing really exists anyway. The line you are referring to says: "I would therefore argue that the way towards total transformation lies less in the perception of the object, and more in the question of existence versus non-existence."'

Gemma raised an eyebrow in Phelan's direction. 'She's quite right,' he said quietly.

Rowanne clapped her hands in almost girlish glee. 'Test me on another, oh, do try me again!'

'No, no, that's fine, we believe you,' Gemma replied.

'I insist.' Rowanne floated across to another bookcase. Show me a book, and I'll get it down for you,' and she started to drift upwards towards one of the upper galleries.

'Oh do stop bobbing up and down like that, you're making me quite seasick,' Fleabag begged.

'I'll choose a book I can reach in the normal way,' Phelan replied, and he pulled a volume from just behind where he was sitting.

'If I tell you the title, you should be able to know what's in it already. Or do you have to hold it first?'

'I've read them all. Just tell me the title.'

'Obscure Parameters of Astrology...' Then he pushed the book back, brushing musty red leather dust from his fingers. 'Look, Rowanne. This is wasting time. We believe you. What did you mean by saying "the Ring Fire cannot fail with me on its side"? That can't be right. The Ring Fire is good and the Blue Magic is evil. The Ring Fire would never want or need help from a wizard.'

Rowanne grinned. 'Look, it's so obvious. You three are so cautious, but the Ring Fire always wins, and now I know all the wizards' secrets, I can let you in on how they are planing to do things, so we cannot possibly fail. I really am going to make a difference for once. I'm going to be *doing* something, instead of standing on the sidelines while you two do all the clever stuff. This time, *I'm* going to be the Champion!'

9

The Three Trials

Later that night, Phelan and Gemma were poring over a parchment scroll containing the three trials of the wizards' Challenge and Fleabag was busy running from bedchamber to bedchamber, testing the respective beds, to see whom he was going to grace with his presence for the night. At last he gave up, sat on the middle of the scroll and began to wash. Just as Phelan was about to put him firmly onto the floor, Kern knocked timidly on the door.

Gemma opened the door and smiled. 'Good to see you, Kern. How are you?'

The boy grunted and shrugged. He wasn't going to start telling *her* how he had spent the afternoon drying out the thick pile of forms he had fished out of the horse trough. He had tried to fill them in but the paper was all stuck together, and the ink had run. He had added to the wetness with a few tears of anger. He was utterly miserable. He had almost not come to the study, but somehow he knew that, enemies or not, they might be kinder to him than anyone else around.

'Come in!' smiled Phelan. 'We have a surprise for

you!' He went to his saddlebag, brought out an oddly shaped bundle wrapped in green velvet and handed it to Kern.

The velvet fell away to reveal his fiddle. His *own* fiddle! But it was expertly mended. The boy looked from Phelan to Gemma and then to the cat in delighted amazement. 'How… Why?' he stuttered.

Gemma laughed. 'We knew how much it meant to you. We were badly delayed setting off for Porthwain, so while we were waiting I asked the palace luthier to look at it for you. He wanted to put another coat of varnish on it, but we didn't have time to wait. If you come our way again, it'll be done.'

'And it's been restrung,' Fleabag added, 'with spun silk from the giant gaudy moth. No cat gut!' he added triumphantly as he jumped onto the table.

Kern's eyes opened as wide as they could possibly go. 'But those are the best strings possible!' He gulped. 'That will cost a fortune, I haven't got that sort of money!' And he put the violin on the table and pushed it reluctantly away from him. 'I can't take it.'

Phelan smiled. 'It's a gift. But if you're really worried about paying, come and play for us one evening.'

Suddenly Kern snatched up the violin and bolted for the door muttering, 'Thanks,' as he ran.

'What's the hurry? Stay and have supper with us,' Gemma urged. 'Play a little now if you'd like. We haven't heard how it sounds with its new strings.'

Kern narrowed his eyes and stared at her suspiciously. 'Why?'

'Why what?' asked Phelan.

'Why should you do this for me? You must want something. Perhaps you think I'm going to betray the

68

wizards to you. Well, I'm not. Not as long as they've got my mother!' and he ran out of the room crying.

'There's an awful lot more to that boy than meets the eye,' Phelan remarked as the door slammed. 'And I would very much like to know what.'

'But meanwhile, we mustn't be distracted from the matter of the Challenge,' Gemma replied. 'We have serious problems ahead.'

'But I'm not sure that Kern *is* a distraction,' Fleabag added. 'Something in my whiskers tells me that he is very important to whatever is going on. In the morning I will ask around and see what I can find out. Obviously, there are no kitchen cats to chat to, and I refuse to sink to the level of asking the butler's dog. But I might allow a few local rats to live if they provide me with information...'

Gemma shook her head. 'You are incorrigible, cat. I am not sure whether I should commend you or berate you for your murderous tactics!'

'Oh commend, of course!' Fleabag exclaimed with a delighted grin. 'I expect at least a second knighthood by the time this adventure is over, and another golden earring, of course... But I think it should have a diamond-studded fieldmouse hanging from it this time, don't you?'

Phelan laughed as he tried to push Fleabag off the parchment scroll that spelled out the Challenge. 'I'm not so sure that the local rodent population would agree with you. Now move, please. We must concentrate. We have only three days to try to work out what the wizards may be up to and to sort out our tactics. Gemma and I have discussed the possibility of refusing to accept the Challenge, but it seems that

Rowanne's acceptance is considered binding, as she is the legal ruler of one of the Kingdom's provinces in her own right. Withdrawing at this stage is apparently the same as conceding defeat. But the good news is that the wizards have agreed to us challenging them as well – although they could hardly have refused.'

'I know the Ring Fire will see us through.' Gemma sighed, 'But I do find it daunting facing hundreds of wizards with nothing more than a shred of trust and a glimmer of light between my fingers.'

'Nothing wrong with that,' Fleabag retorted. 'Anyway, what does the parchment say? Let's know the worst before we start worrying.'

'Well, if you move your fur, I can read it,' Phelan replied.

Fleabag sniffed and moved.

'Day one,' Phelan read, running his finger along the line of ornate, illuminated script: *'The trial of strength. Each contestant may challenge the opponent to a trial of physical skill and stamina.'*

'Have you any idea what that will be?' Gemma asked.

'Yes, they've told me: it's broadsword fighting.'

Gemma shook her head and Fleabag turned as pale as a black cat can. 'Do you think we dare ask Rowanne to take that trial for us? She's the greatest swordfighter in the Kingdom, without a doubt.'

Phelan sat back in his chair and bit his lip. 'I know, but I'm not sure I want Rowanne doing anything for us at the moment. Do you? It's not that I don't trust her, it's just that... well, she doesn't *feel* like Rowanne anymore.'

Gemma opened her hands where the small glimmer of golden Ring Fire burned in each palm. 'I just can't believe she's turned evil – not *wholly*. She's just infatuated with the idea of power and is being very silly...'

'But what induced her to accept the Challenge on our behalf anyway? Do you think it was really so the Ring Fire could win once and for all as she says, or was there some other motive? Where are her loyalties? Would she be fighting for us or...' Phelan hesitated. 'I've just had an awful thought. Do you think she might, willingly or unwillingly, be the *wizards'* champion? She's so famous they must know that no knight or soldier in the Kingdom could beat her.'

Gemma and Phelan exchanged worried glances, but Fleabag just began to scratch, sending fleas all over the place. 'Speak for yourself. I'd match my claws against a rusty old broadsword any day of the week! In fact, give me leave, Phelan, and *I'll* be your champion.'

Phelan's face broke into a broad grin. From where he was seated he swept a bow from the waist. 'Sir Scrag-Belly, what king could expect a more noble offer? My only reason for refusing you is that it might be argued that the match would be unequal.'

Fleabag grinned back. 'You mean she might be daunted by having me as a foe? Spoken like a true and honourable King, Sire. However, I have always wanted to repay a few personal debts owed to the Princess, and the opportunity would give me great pleasure...'

'But what if it *isn't* Rowanne?' Gemma asked

earnestly. 'What if it is some other knight? He or she might complain that your multitude of claws was unfair against one mere iron sword?'

'True,' conceded Fleabag. 'It will have to be you then, Phelan.'

The King nodded. 'I suppose so. I have worked hard at learning sword skills but I don't know if I will be good enough. Anyway, if I live through that round, I'll challenge them to running. I was always pretty good at that. And if their champion *is* Rowanne, I'll win. She can never get her breathing right in a full-length race.'

'But we still don't know for certain that she'll be working against us,' Gemma added sadly.

'We must be practical,' the King added. 'We don't know she is working entirely *for* us either, despite all the things she was saying about finding out the wizards' secrets to use against them.'

Gemma looked sadly down into her hands where two tiny points of the Ring Fire burned. 'I wish I could understand what the Fire is saying. It looks so very calm at the moment. I wish it would *tell* me something!'

'It will, in good time,' Phelan smiled, turning to the parchment again. 'Ah, now, Fleabag, here *is* something you can do – *the trial of wisdom*!'

Fleabag raised a whiskery eyebrow. For all his pomposity, he had never thought of himself as being particularly wise. 'You're kidding, of course!' he muttered, slightly apprehensively. 'Gemma or you ought to do that one.'

'No. I'm absolutely serious,' Phelan replied, looking straight at the cat with a very determined expression. 'In any argument, you are the one with all the clever answers. Your tongue is even sharper than your claws. You're quite a wise old hearthrug, you know!'

Fleabag still looked worried. He was not quite certain whether the King was mocking him or not, but ever since the day when they had first met, and Phelan had swung Fleabag by the tail, the cat had always treated his friend with genuine respect.

'What will I have to do? I'm not a great reader, and if someone like Rowanne starts spouting quotations at us like she did earlier, I'm lost!'

'No, I think it will probably be riddles, although they can choose book learning if they want... Just a minute, it says here... blah, blah, blah... yes, riddles it is. *The most noble and ancient art of word cunning.* That's a posh name for riddles, isn't it? Do you know any?'

'One or two,' the cat replied dubiously. 'I'll do it, because you've done me the honour of asking, as my King and all that... but I'll have you know, I'm not happy, not happy at all.' And he jumped down from the table and began to walk towards Gemma's bedroom with drooping head and loosely hanging tail.

Gemma ran after him and picked him up to scratch behind his ears. 'Cheer up, old friend. I'll keep you surrounded by the Ring Fire the whole time. I'm sure the Fire Giver will give you all the wisdom you could ever need. What will your Challenge to them be?'

Fleabag momentarily lost his anxious look and smirked. 'I will set them a puzzle – how to get out of a locked room filled with the fleas of a hundred camels. Beyond that there will be a locked room with the lice of a thousand camel-drivers, then beyond that there will be a locked room with the mange of a hundred thousand mongrel dogs. They have to escape it all with one movement. How?'

Gemma looked amazed and laughed. 'I've no idea, how?'

Fleabag sniffed contemptuously, jumped down and slunk away. 'You'll have to wait to find out. I'm not telling *you*. If you can't work that one out, I can see why the King realized that I am obviously the best choice for this task!' and he disappeared under the hanging folds of the tablecloth.

'You get out by jumping out of the window, that's an old one!' laughed Phelan. Then, as Gemma sat down, he looked serious. 'Day three, of course is the trial of magical powers. It will be you, or more rightly the Ring Fire against the Blue Magic. Once and for all.'

Gemma leaned her elbows on the table in front of her and hunched her shoulders. Despite three years of working with the Ring Fire, and slowly beginning to understand its ways, the thought of situations like this still terrified her and made her feel small and inadequate. 'This is the one Rowanne really wants to fight for us, isn't it?' she asked miserably. 'She thinks that by learning the secrets of the Blue Magic she can help us... Do you think she really believes it?'

Phelan leaned back and looked at the ceiling. 'Yes, I do. But I also think she's wrong. She can't possibly fight for the Ring Fire with the Blue Magic inside her. It can't be done. She'll have to choose.'

Gemma opened her right hand and stared long

and hard at the Ring Fire. 'I don't know what we are going to do, but I know *I* shouldn't fight that battle. I'm certain the Ring Fire has other ideas about how that trial will be met. *My* job is to wait, and watch the Fire burn. Oh, that's the most difficult thing of all – to do nothing!'

And she buried her tired head in her arms. From somewhere outside, the strains of a violin playing a familiar melody seeped in through the shutters.

10

An Offer of Help

For the next two days, Fleabag read every book of
riddles he could find, although in the ends of his
whiskers and in the tip of his tail he felt that swot-
ting up on witty lines wasn't going to save the day.
He was very nervous.

Rowanne often met him in the library, floating up
and down in her spooky way, offering him this book
and that. But her presence only made him feel
uncomfortable, so on the third day he slunk off to
the roof tiles where even she did not follow him.
There he sat in the wintry sun, peering down at the
practice yards below.

There Phelan was working himself into an uncomfortable sweat training with his sergeant at arms.

Just watching all that exercise made Fleabag tired,
so he curled up and snuggled his nose under his
matted tail. He decided that a well-rested head was
probably better than one full of words from wizard's
books. Tomorrow would come when it was time to for
it to do so. He would let the Ring Fire do the worrying.

Far below Phelan rested on the pommel of his
sword and panted. He wiped sweat from his face

with his handkerchief and winced. The muscles on the back of his neck were knotted and swollen. Every sinew in his arms and legs screamed for rest. He had worked left- and right-handed, with broadsword in one hand, and dagger in the other, then changing, left to right, right to left. He'd tried every sword that he and his sergeant had with him. Nothing felt quite right somehow: the balance was wrong, the hilt was too long or short or the haft was out of true. In the end he felt irritable and tired.

His favourite blade was in the armoury at home. If he had guessed what Rowanne was up to he'd have brought it with him. But he had thought this was going to be a diplomatic mission.

Just as he was about to give up, Rowanne stepped out into the bright winter sunshine of the courtyard. For once, she was dressed in knightly gear of steel armour strapped over a red woollen doublet rather than the long flowing dark- and light-blue robes that made her look so eerily unlike herself.

Without saying a word, she unsheathed her own sword, knelt and handed it to the King, hilt first. 'My sword is yours, my Lord,' she said at last. 'Really,' she added, looking him directly in the eye. 'Take it, it's better than any of the others here. It's your only chance.'

Phelan hesitated. For once, the blue seemed to be fading from the Princess' skin, and almost the flush of her old brown tan seemed to appear across her cheeks. The King took the sword.

'It's all right,' the Princess assured him as she stood. 'It won't bite and it's not enchanted or anything. It's just a very good sword, probably a little light for you, but that's a good thing because you're over-tired.' Then she took one of the other swords that Phelan had been working with and raised it between her eyes in salute. 'Can I help you practice? I can see exactly what you are doing wrong…'

Phelan looked at her. This wasn't magic. This was friendship and loyalty. 'Thank you, I'd be grateful.' He bowed slightly.

Then for the next hour he worked as he had never worked before, sweeping this way and that as the Princess showed her true skill as a warrior – the skill that had once made her a member of the old Queen's bodyguard and one of the most valued knights in Phelan's Kingdom.

As the sun began to lose height and the air began to chill, Rowanne flopped down on a bale of hay and smiled.

It was the old, true Rowanne who was there, with normal blue eyes and deep-tanned skin from her outdoor life. Her grasp was honest and firm as she shook Phelan's hand. 'You will fight well tomorrow. I've managed to discover who they are putting against you in the fight. It's a knight called Grimbold, and he's not a wizard! But watch his left foot. He uses it when you least expect it.'

Then she dropped her gaze and stared at the point of her sword, which she used to scratch the emblem of the Ring Fire on one of the cobbles at her feet.

'I do know what I'm doing,' she said, looking at Phelan again. 'Although I don't know whether I'll live through this. But whatever you see me do, or hear me say, please remember I'm doing it all for the Ring Fire. Someone's got to stand up and face the

Blue Magic once and for all, and I'm proud it's me.'

'But not like this,' Phelan began. 'Come and see Gemma and let us help you get rid of the Blue Magic that's taking you over. We can all get through this together, but joining the ranks of the enemy isn't the way. It never has been...'

Suddenly Rowanne turned her head, although Phelan heard no one calling. 'I must go now. Remember what I said about Grimbold.'

Then she saluted the King formally with her sword and turned away. As she did so, she lifted her helmet from her head and pulled off her woollen under-cap, letting her hair tumble over her shoulders. All the blue had gone; it was dark brown again.

Then she turned back and smiled. 'You will use the sword, won't you? Promise!' And she ran inside.

Phelan could not find Gemma in their suite of rooms. He didn't go and look for her because he ached so much all he wanted was a hot bath. Anyway, perhaps it was best to have a quiet think about the changes in Rowanne before he told Gemma his suspicions. If only there was some way of distracting the Princess from the Blue Magic before the Challenge began.

Phelan stayed in his bath for a full hour, trying to remember what Rowanne had taught him about swordsmanship. He would never be a master, he knew that, but he would do his best, and hope that Rowanne was right about Grimbold not being a wizard. He was grateful for the Princess' sword. It was a good one. Although it was a little light and short, it felt as though it belonged in his hand.

As he soaked, he decided that he would save some

of his strength from the sword fight for the trial he had set for the wizards – a long sprint. He knew he had a chance to win that. If he exhausted himself in the fight, then lost the race because he was over-tired, he would throw everything away. The best he could hope for was a draw.

The ultimate fate of the Kingdom rested on the trial of magic – the Ring Fire against the wizards' blue power – and although the Ring Fire was indisputably the stronger, would they carry it well, allowing it to flow as it would? Had the whole way the Challenges had come about forced the Ring Fire into a bad position? If this battle was lost, would it mean more Challenges and maybe even wars in the future?

Gemma had steadfastly refused to accept the magical trial, and Rowanne equally steadfastly kept offering to fight the contest on Gemma's behalf. As soon as she left Phelan in the practice yard, Rowanne had changed into her wizard's robes again and cornered Gemma in the library. Her skin had regained its blue tinge almost as soon as she had taken off her armour and turned her thoughts back to magical things. It was as if the real Rowanne was hung in the armoury lockers along with the steel plate greaves and cuirasses, the leather straps and the burnished shields. But the blue-haired woman with purple fingernails was oblivious to her own changes.

Gemma gulped as Rowanne floated along the great room, arms wide, as if to enfold her old friend in an affectionate hug.

'I do wish you wouldn't *do* that,' Gemma muttered, ducking the outstretched blue arms.

'Do what?' Rowanne asked in amazement, not a

little hurt at Gemma's evasion.

'*Float* like that. It's disconcerting. What happened to the old Rowanne who liked solid floors, a sturdy horse and a cold iron sword in her hand?'

'But I've changed, Gemma dear. Only for the better, I assure you. I've seen how futile the old ways of fighting for fighting's sake really are. Life is so much more *subtle* than that. Swords are playthings for children.'

'Tell that to the wizards,' Gemma retorted.

'What do you mean?'

'We have been challenged to a sword fight tomorrow, in case you've forgotten – or didn't they tell you what the specific trials were?'

Rowanne tossed her indigo-black hair and laughed lightly. 'Oh that – that's just a formality. I've been helping Phelan train this afternoon, but that's not the serious trial.'

'So we don't have to do it?' Gemma sounded hopeful. There was no point Phelan risking life and limb at the hands of some bloodthirsty knight, probably with an enchanted sword, if it wasn't strictly necessary.

'On the contrary. Three trials are the rule, and three trials must be fought. It's the law.'

'But we didn't accept the Challenge – you did, on our behalf. Why should we fight at all?' Gemma was angry. She felt tricked into the whole situation.

'But you know that I did it for the glory of the Ring Fire so that these silly disputes should be ended, once and for all.' Rowanne smiled condescendingly, 'Anyway, if you don't fight, you'll be deemed to have conceded. Come, be sensible, let me fight the magical trial on your behalf. In fact, if I take on your likeness, no one need even know it's me. I know this terrific transformation spell that makes me look just like you. Even old M'Kinnik doesn't know the difference. I tried it on him for almost half an hour this morning, and he kept talking to me as if I were you. I had to excuse myself in the end, it was getting awkward.'

'You did *what*?' Gemma was furious. 'How dare you impersonate me? You had no right...'

'Calm down,' Rowanne laughed. 'I know what I'm doing. I managed to discover who they're putting against you in the sword fight. I've told Phelan all about him already. It's a knight called Grimbold who's as human as you or I...'

At this Gemma glanced across at her old friend and winced. Rowanne's blueness was getting disconcerting, although she seemed unaware of it. The Fire Wielder shook her head. 'Please stop all this nonsense, Rowanne. Come home and we will see what wisdom the Ring Fire has to fight the wizards on its own terms. The more involved you get in this magic nonsense, the more blue you become, and the more oblivious you are to the truth!'

Rowanne looked at Gemma with total incomprehension. 'What *are* you talking about? *Me, blue*? Look...' and she stretched her arm next to Gemma's own. Gemma winced and wanted to pull her arm away, for a wave of icy blueness blushed across the Princess' skin as they compared arms.

'I'm every bit as pink as you – perhaps a little browner, but that's because of the outdoor life I used to lead.'

'You can't see it, can you?' Gemma gasped, jumping up. Now she was certain she wanted Rowanne to be no part of the Ring Fire's response to the Challenge. 'You really are totally unaware of what's happening to you!' and she started to run out of the library.

'Wait! If you won't let me fight for you, at least let me advise you, I know what spell they are intending to use on the third day...'

But Gemma had gone. She ran along corridor after corridor, heading towards the study and trying very hard not to cry. Her friend was rapidly being taken over by the Blue Magic, for which there was probably no cure. She was certain they were fighting senseless battles in which they would probably all die.

The Ring Fire *would* win, she was still certain of that, but she had no idea how – or when. It all seemed so senseless and such a waste. Suddenly, she had an urge to go outside and breathe some air. She pushed at the nearest door that looked as if it might lead outside.

But although sunlight streamed into the narrow passageway as the door creaked on its hinges, what she saw made her stop in her tracks.

11

Within the Flames

The door did not lead outside, but to a small circular room with a dozen lancet windows, allowing a stream of yellow sunshine to spill across the floor. On the far side of the room was a wide-spanning carved stone fireplace, cut to look like a forest of intertwining trees. In the grate burned a warm, welcoming blaze of golden flames. But in the middle of the fire lay the figure of a shabby young woman.

Kern was kneeling in the grate, trying to stretch his hands through the flames to take hold of the woman. He was talking rapidly, and although he could not touch her it was clear he was trying to get her out.

Gemma ran forwards and tried to grasp the woman's wrist, but the fire was too hot. She jumped back and rubbed her arms, brushing her skirt in case the flames had caught the cloth. It was then she realized that the woman seemed to be quite contentedly asleep. The flames did not appear to burn her, nor even to make her hot or scorched. Her fair skin looked quite cool and comfortable. She looked so peaceful she could easily have been lying in the middle of a grassy field with her long brown hair spread out amongst wild flowers instead of white and black ashes.

Kern looked up at Gemma, tears streaming down his ashy face. 'Do some of your fire magic, *please!* It's my mother! It's Claire!' Then he pulled his shirt sleeves down over his wrists and tried to tug again; 'Come *on*, Mother, get out of that fire! You'll get burned! Wake up and we'll both escape. They'll not keep either of us here any longer. Tell her, Gemma, tell her I've done all the wizards said, and we're both free!' And with that he collapsed in an exhausted heap on an old tapestry rug that covered the floor and started to sob.

Gemma knelt next to Kern and peered at the figure. Suddenly it struck Gemma that Kern's mother was not at all like him. He was a wide-cheek-boned westerner like one of the old wizards... but this was no time to think of such matters. Once again she put her hands out towards the sleeping figure, but drew them back very quickly. As she stared into the flames, a warm feeling spread through her own arms and face and she realized how cold she had become during the afternoon.

Claire did not stir, except to breathe gently. She was still unharmed by the fire. 'I wonder if this is real, or another sending?' Gemma murmured to herself, looking hard for any clues. 'How long has she been like this?' she asked, sitting back on her heels.

'I don't know,' the boy replied, choked by a voice that was trying not to cry. 'I found her an hour or so ago, I suppose. She seems to be stuck somehow. I'm sure it's magic, and I will kill the next wizard I see, I swear! They have lied to me at every turn and I *will* be avenged. I will kill them all!' he bellowed, rising to his feet and clenching his fists in fury.

'Hush!' warned Gemma. 'Not so loud. I will do what I can, but I'm going to need help. Run quickly and fetch Phelan. He will either be in the practice yard, or in our rooms. I'll try to find Fleabag. Meet me here as soon as you can. Oh, and ask Phelan to bring my cloak.'

With that Gemma slipped back inside the long corridor. Kern ran past her, as soft and silent as a shadow. Gemma soon found a small understairs broom cupboard where she could open her hands and let the Ring Fire burn safely. She had to think, and she needed help against this spell – whatever it was. As she looked into the tiny flame within her palm, the Ring Fire's golden glow seemed to be burning very brightly.

She felt calm, and almost happy. But she could not think of a way to help Kern's mother. It seemed that the Ring Fire wasn't interested. That made her angry.

'Oh, where is Fleabag?' she found herself asking out loud. 'Why is he always under my feet when I don't want him, and never here when he's needed the most? He could be anywhere in this rabbit-warren of halls and passageways, and there are so many buildings here. Oh, where do I start?'

Suddenly a warm, purring rub of fur against her leg made her jump.

'Did somebody call?' Fleabag whispered as he jumped into his friend's arms.

The sudden weight of the cat made Gemma

stumble back against the brooms and brushes. 'What are you doing here?' she gasped as the cat rubbed his nose hard under her chin.

'I thought you wanted me,' Fleabag replied. 'I'll go away again if I'm *not* wanted. I was just about to pounce on a nice bit of supper when I heard you take my name in vain. I bet I've lost it now – as juicy a bit of fresh house mouse as you could wish for!' And he wriggled to get down.

But Gemma had him firmly by the scruff of the neck. 'Oh no, you don't. I was just wondering out loud where you were, that's all. But now I've got you, you aren't going to escape. Someone needs your help more than you need your supper!'

'I can't imagine anything could be as important as that!' the cat replied. 'Anyway, what are you doing skulking in a dark cupboard like a field shrew caught indoors? I thought you were the great Fire Wielder, scared of no one?'

'This is no time for jokes,' Gemma said urgently. 'Although I must admit, dreadful company that you are, I am more than pleased to see you.' She told him briefly about the strange figure in the fireplace who wasn't burned by the fire. 'The flames are real enough, and I can't get near her. I wondered if she's another sending, but she *seems* very real. I've sent Kern to find Phelan and to bring my cloak. Perhaps we can wrap our arms in it to try to rescue the poor woman. The next problem will be getting her back to our rooms without being noticed. Come and see what you think.'

Gemma led her friend back along the shadowy corridor until they reached the door. Gemma opened it cautiously and a blast of icy air blew in, carrying flurries of wet snow with it. Dark night had fallen. There was no sunlit little room with a roaring fire under a wide stone mantelpiece.

'Brrr!' moaned Fleabag. 'I've only just come in from the roof tiles. Now I've got to go out again!'

'This is strange,' Gemma murmured, stepping outside into a cobbled yard. 'I'm certain there was a room here, only a few moments ago.' The door slammed behind her as the wind whipped her hair against her face and the snow caught in her eyes so she could barely see.

Just then, the sound of the door handle being turned behind them made Gemma and the cat flatten themselves against the wall and hold their breath. Suddenly the wind caught the door and flung it open, almost knocking Gemma flying, but she bit her tongue and tried to stay out of sight.

To her relief it was Kern and Phelan, with Gemma's cloak.

Kern looked around the courtyard, and it seemed to Gemma as if he was trying not to cry. 'Where is she?' he begged, 'Please tell me where she is! What have you done with my mother?' he demanded. 'You're as tricky as those wizards, you've magicked her away! I knew I shouldn't trust you. You killed my father and my brothers, now you've burned her to death too. I'll kill you, I'll...' and he ran across to Gemma and began to kick and thump her.

Phelan grabbed at the lad. 'Steady, can't you see? Gemma doesn't know what's going on any more than you or I do. But I have an idea, and if I'm right, your mother's quite safe – safer than we are at the moment! Come inside and let's talk.'

The friends led the frightened boy back into the hallway. 'Do you think we just went to the wrong doorway?' Gemma asked.

'No,' Phelan replied, peering cautiously around. 'You *and* Kern wouldn't have both taken the wrong door. From what Kern tells me, there's more to it than that. Fleabag, run ahead and warn us if you see any wizards coming. Kern, trust us. At least long enough to talk this over. Now, which is the quickest way back to our rooms?'

Kern pointed along the corridor and shuddered. It was empty but it looked terribly long and dark. The servants had not yet lit the torches in the sconces. How would they ever get to the end of it, let alone reach safety? The cat slid around a bend and disappeared. Kern led Gemma and Phelan swiftly to the left, then they sank into a gloomy niche where Fleabag was already waiting for them. Kern flattened himself against the wall to peer around the next corner.

'Back!' hissed the cat. 'I smell a wizard!' He slipped into the farthest corner of the recess and curled up very small so he looked like an even blacker part of the black shadows.

Phelan opened the wide folds of the cloak, pushed Kern and Gemma underneath and thrust them to the back of the recess. 'Don't move!' he warned. Then stepping out into the corridor he stooped down and turned his back to the approaching figure.

The wizard marched on with a heavy tread then, as she drew close to the friends, her steps hesitated and slowed.

'What are you doing here at this hour, boy?' she demanded in a deep voice. 'It is almost time for the Great Convocation. This area should have been cleaned hours ago.'

Phelan half rose, then bowed, keeping his head well down as he tugged at his forelock and replied in a gruff voice. 'Beggin' your pardon, your Holiness, t'was a spillage an' all.'

'A spillage?' the woman demanded. 'What do you mean?'

'T'was a spillage of beans an' lentils, Ma'am.'

'Beans and lentils? What are you talking about, boy?'

'I don' know how they came to be here, Ma'am. I jus' knows they was 'ere an' I bin sent to pick 'em up, so please, your Holiness.' And he bowed again.

The wizard stepped forward and grabbed at Phelan's chin and tugged his beard forward so she could look at his face. At the same time she lit a magical blue flame between her fingers.

But before she could register who she was looking at, Phelan drew back his fist and punched the wizard in the nose. 'Run!' he hissed to the others. 'That was not well done. They will all be after us now.'

With that he tugged the cloak over his shoulder as he fled, leading the group up the next staircase and onto the landing above. Gemma suddenly stopped dead. 'Oh no! My hands! Why does the Ring Fire *do* this to me?' and she held out her hands as tongues of Ring Fire flashed out in the shadowy corridor. Just at that second, a group of giggling servant girls brushed past them, and Phelan spread the cloak over Gemma, covering her from top to toe.

The girls threw odd looks as they squeezed to one side. But as they moved, one of them caught the cloak against her arm. The heavy cloth fell back, revealing Gemma's fiery hands. All the girls fell silent and made the sign against the evil eye as they turned their faces to the wall, holding their breath until the company was past.

Suddenly a terrible screeching noise and a flap of wings made everyone look up. The servants screamed and ran, disappearing up an iron staircase and through a heavy wooden door which they slammed behind them.

Gemma, Phelan and Kern were left facing a huge bird, black as night with a wingspan that swept the stone walls either side of the narrow passage. Its beak was icy blue and its eyes were piercing azure sapphires that made the watchers shiver with dread.

'How did *that* get inside?' Gemma gasped, eyes wide. Wherever the crows flew, the wizards were never far behind.

'I don't know, but I think we ought to run!' Phelan urged.

Fleabag yowled and hissed and slashed upwards with his front claws, balancing precariously on his one remaining back leg as he tried to rake the belly of the mage-creature with his dagger-points.

Kern ducked as the creature swung around in the width of the stairwell to take another swoop. This time its talons were extended towards the cowering figures. It did not seem to be after any particular one of them, but it struck terror as it flew.

As the creature passed, Phelan was able to straighten himself enough to draw Rowanne's sword and get a good balance. As the huge crow turned again, Phelan knew he had only a few seconds to plan his defence. He carefully watched the way the bird moved, and anticipated how it would attack. He breathed deeply, waiting as the great bird loomed towards them.

It was almost on them again, screeching with its deadly, razor sharp beak wide open, and talons ready to gouge and rip.

Gemma raised her hands, but the Ring Fire had faded. Her hands were quite empty. 'Where *has* it gone?' she exclaimed in horror, cowering behind Phelan. 'Why is it never there when I need it most?'

'Quick!' hissed Fleabag. 'Our quarters are just along there, first corridor to the right, then left at the end. Go!' Gemma dared not look back, but she ducked as another terrible screech signalled the arrival of the creature's mate from above the stairwell.

The first bird swooped down and scraped Fleabag's back with its deadly talons, just as Phelan leaped up, plunging Rowanne's sword hilt deep in the night-blue feathers until hot blood drenched his arm.

The King fell under the weight of the dying creature, and it took all of Kern's strength to heave the corpse aside before Phelan could wrest his sword from the tangle of blood and feathers.

Gemma swept the bleeding Fleabag into her arms as she turned to flee. She glanced back for one second, and saw Phelan and Kern staring in horror as the second bird landed and began to devour her own mate, tugging strips of flesh from the still-warm corpse.

Phelan moved quietly to where Kern crouched. 'Do everything very slowly. Don't frighten the bird,' Phelan warned, as he edged along the wall.

Fighting a dreadful feeling that she was going to be sick, Gemma ran.

12

Kern's Story

As Gemma flung open the door to their darkened rooms, her heart was pounding and she could hardly breathe. Sweat dripped down her face and into her eyes.

The study was quite dark, except for a faint bluish glow from the bookshelves and a dull red glimmer from a dying fire in the grate. Gemma laid Fleabag gently down on a towel and went to look at the eerie light. 'Of course,' she muttered. 'They're *wizards'* books! Ugh,' she shuddered, 'that blue colour gives me the creeps.'

Just then, the sound of Phelan and Kern clattering through the door made Gemma spring into action.

Without thinking about finding the tinder box, Gemma touched each of the lamps with her fingers, so they burned with the glow from the Ring Fire. Then she stirred up the dying fire in the grate. The warmth of the clear light made everyone feel better.

Gemma fetched warm water to bathe Fleabag's wounds. 'You're lucky, they're only light scratches. How do you feel, old friend?' she asked kindly.

'Sore,' the cat replied. 'It isn't bad enough to give

me a decent hero's death, but I'll need pampering and a great deal of fish and sympathy for a few weeks if I'm to make a full recovery.'

Gemma laughed as she carried him into her bedroom to sleep.

Back in the study, supper had been left out for them. Phelan pulled out a chair and made Kern sit. 'I will tell you what I think is happening to your mother, but I must eat first,' he said. 'I need to revive my wits before I do anything.'

Kern was fidgety, and kept throwing suspicious sidelong glances at Phelan and Gemma, but he too ate and said nothing. It was not long before only crumbs were left, and a rather stiff and bedraggled Fleabag decided that he needed nourishment too.

'Hello, Fleabag. Nice to see you. How are you feeling?' Phelan laughed, and put a plate loaded with fish on the floor for him to eat.

'Miserable!' the cat replied. 'They've *only* got fresh cream and smoked salmon for my tea.' Then the incorrigible animal picked up the fish from his plate and jumped behind the settee to eat it.

'Oh you'll live!' Phelan laughed.

Fleabag stopped eating, licked his whiskers and peered around the edge of the settee looking serious for once. 'I don't know how that thing caught me, but his talons were *sharp*, then I just went all cold. The next thing I knew, I was in here feeling warm as toast with a nice comforting circle of friends all around me, and supper laid out, just as it should be for a cat of my rank. Pity it wasn't the lightly grilled field mouse on toast I ordered. Then my bliss would have been complete.'

Gemma scratched her old friend behind the ear,

enjoying the way the firelight caught on his earring. 'Nothing to be ashamed of. Still, the warmth of the Ring Fire seems to have done you some good, even if it hasn't mended your table manners. You've spilled cream all over that cushion.'

Suddenly Kern could contain himself no longer. 'Look, I've been patient with you all,' he snapped, 'and now I want to know what's going on. Why didn't you help me get my mother away from that horrid fire, and why did you magic that room away when my back was turned? I should never have left you. You tricked me out of the room... you...'

'Calm down,' Phelan said gently. 'Listen to what I *think* happened. Although I wasn't there, I do have an idea. You know you said the room was bright and warm, even though it was dark, cold and already snowing outside?'

'Yes,' Kern replied, hesitantly. 'What of it? Things are rarely as they seem around here. That's nothing.'

'Yes, but you know some magic, Kern; was it real or a spell?'

Kern hesitated before answering. 'It was... real... I think.'

Phelan nodded. 'Yet the courtyard was real, too, wasn't it? Not an illusion?'

The boy nodded again.

'And Gemma, when you put your hands into the fire, what happened?'

'It burned me,' she replied, looking at her hands. Then she hesitated. 'No, it didn't. It just hurt a bit, but I've got no blisters or anything... How strange!'

'And how did Kern's mother look?' the King persisted.

96

'Well, content, and comfortable too!' she added, as light began to dawn.

'What *are* you talking about?' Kern demanded, thumping the table with his fist. 'You're all talking in riddles, worse than any wizard! I saw my mother being burned alive in a huge fire and you did nothing to help her, Gemma. Then she was magicked away. This is all too much. What *is* happening?' he demanded.

From behind the settee Fleabag chuckled. 'Oh Kern, you should have a cat's brain in your head, as well as cat-guts for strings. Then you might see what's at the very end of your nose.'

Kern looked put out, and his foot twitched as if he longed to boot Fleabag. 'What *are* you talking about?' he muttered.

Fleabag purred, tried to roll over, and remembered he couldn't because of the great bird's scratches on his back. 'The Ring Fire has her. She's safe. Safer than she has ever been in all her life.'

'But where was the room? Wasn't that a wizards' trick?'

'Oh that's real, all right,' Phelan assured the boy. 'But it's no *place* in particular. It's everywhere and anywhere, wherever the Fire Giver wants to put it. You were just being shown that she is safe, and being told not to worry.'

Kern frowned. 'But if it *was* the Ring Fire, why did it hurt Gemma's hands?' he asked.

'To warn her not to interfere,' Phelan replied. 'To tell Gemma she had to leave your mother where she was.'

This did not comfort Kern at all. He jumped to

his feet and stood glaring in front of Phelan, 'But how are we going to get her back? What are you going to do to rescue her from this Ring Fire of yours?'

'We don't need to,' the King said quietly. 'Your mother is asleep somewhere, safe, and well cared for. When the Fire Giver knows the time is right, your mother will waken, and you will find her. You just have to trust!'

Kern went bright red in the face and thumped the table again. 'Trust! Trust! Why should I trust you, when you're all talking such nonsense. I don't care if *you're* a King, and *you're* a Fire Wielder and *you're* a cat of ninety-nine lives...'

'One hundred and ninety-nine,' Fleabag put in with a grin.

Kern didn't even stop to scowl at the cat. 'This is ridiculous. I want my mother back. What's the difference between your magic and the wizards'? Only the colour, as far as I can see. And that means nothing!'

Gemma held open her hand and let the Ring Fire burn gently. 'Look into it,' she said quietly. 'How does it make you feel?'

Kern said nothing, but stared open-mouthed at the gentle, gold flame. Then Gemma got up and picked up one of the books that had been glowing blue before she had lit the lamps. 'And now look at something that carries the wizards' magic...'

Kern took the book, and dropped it, immediately, kicking it across the room. 'I don't want to look at it – it's horrid!' he muttered, hanging his head. 'Well, perhaps the Ring Fire isn't so bad... You think it's taken her to look after her while things are too dangerous here?'

'Exactly,' said Phelan.

'I suppose it could make sense.' Kern sat down again and looked thoughtful. 'If M'Kinnik thought I was about to claim my freedom, he might have tried to hide my mother to keep us here. He knows I would never dream of leaving without her.'

Phelan leaned back in his chair and sipped at his wine. 'If your mother was taken by the Ring Fire to a safe place, the wizards aren't about to admit that, so they let you think they've hidden her. But talking of trust, isn't it about time we knew a little about you? Who *are* you? Why are you and your mother so important to the University? The Ring Fire went to great lengths to protect your mother.'

Kern reddened and shrugged as he began to kick at the table leg. 'How should I know? I'd never heard of your Ring Fire before I came to Harflorum.'

Phelan noticed the evaded question and leaned forward as he tried to look Kern in the eye. 'But why did you come to Harflorum in the first place? And what was all that about "doing everything the wizards said"?'

The boy sighed, and stared into the golden firelight in the grate. It was soft and gentle, like the Fire that was caring for his mother. 'I was told that my mother and I would be free to leave here for ever if I did an errand for the wizards… I had to go to Harflorum and find the last carrier of the pure Blue Magic and bring him or her back here… But when I got back, Mother had disappeared. Until today I thought the wizards had taken her.'

'They may have done,' Gemma replied. 'But whatever happened, the Ring Fire has her now, and that is the important thing.'

'How could I have been so *stupid* as to have believed the wizards?' Kern went on. 'Especially M'Kinnik! He was my father's friend. I thought he meant me well.'

'But who was your father?' Gemma asked, hoping not to hear the answer she dreaded.

Kern sighed. 'The Chancellor of All Wizards, whom you killed in the Hall of Light three years ago,' he replied, looking Gemma directly in the face.

Gemma hung her head. 'Oh, I'm – I'm sorry…'

'Don't be!' Kern smiled ruefully. 'Mother was forced to marry. She was given to the University in lieu of rent on my grandfather's farm. She was not wanted by my father. Neither was I. Let's face it, what wizard of the Blue Magic wants a *seventh* son? They are supposed to be omens for good. The main reason my father married my mother was some weird idea that she was going to give him a daughter. There were already two older girls in the family, but third daughters for wizards are considered something rather special.

'So when I was born a boy, my father never spoke to either of us again. I was always considered to be a nuisance and in the way. My older brothers and sisters had no time for me, except Domnall. He was always very kind,' Kern said. 'He gave me my violin and treated me like a brother… That meant a lot to me.'

Gemma stared at the floor and bit her lip. 'I didn't exactly kill either of them, you know. They both got caught up in their own spells. I didn't mean anyone any harm. I just wanted both your father and your brothers to stop using magic for evil ends. In fact we tried to ban the use of magic altogether after the Battle of Porthwain, but it didn't work. I suppose that was too much to expect.'

'I thought you were the evil one,' Kern said quietly. 'I had sworn that once I had delivered the carrier of the Blue Magic to the wizards and Mother and I were free, I would have my vengeance on you. But I was wrong. You were only fighting for what was right and, as you say, my father, Sethan and Domnall all became entangled in evil of their own making. I can see that now. I'm sorry...' and he held out his hand in friendship.

But just as he did so, the flames in the torches around the room flickered and sank to mere pinpricks of light and the room went very cold.

Gemma sprang to her feet and looked around wildly. 'What's happening?' she gulped.

'We're under attack!' Phelan said, jumping to his feet. 'But how, and where?'

Gemma turned to Kern. 'Phelan and I must go and see what we can find out. Please, fetch your violin and play the air I heard you trying out the other evening... the Ring Fire song from the Fire Festival. It will help us think. Songs and music are very important to help keep the Ring Fire bright in our minds.'

Kern nodded. 'I'll get it straight away,' and he left the room, with Fleabag close behind him.

Silently he slipped along the dark corridors, looking carefully this way and that, darting from shadow to shadow as the wan blue light from the torches along the way guttered and flared in the uncertain draughts.

'How brave are you, Fleabag?' Kern asked the cat. 'There is a short cut if we turn left here, but it involves going along the gallery at the top of the Great Hall.'

Fleabag puffed himself up so his tail turned to a bottlebrush and his whiskers splayed as wide as they would go. 'I am the *epitome* of courage, my dear boy. After all, I am the cat who took on your father single-pawed – well, almost,' he muttered quietly under his breath. 'I suppose Gemma and Phelan did help a bit at times...' And he followed the boy through the small door that led out onto the balcony, his eyes glowing like coach lamps in the dark.

Kern stooped low, so as not to be seen from below, and he moved swiftly and stealthily, reaching the far door within only one or two heartbeats.

Fleabag, however, jumped up onto the balustrade and surveyed the scene below.

Kern was white with terror. 'Get *down*!' he hissed, flapping urgently with his hands. 'They'll turn you into a mouse as soon as look at you!'

But Fleabag sat quite calmly where he was. 'I don't think they will,' he said. 'They've got other things on their minds. Come and look at this...'

13

The Return of the Fire Maiden

The vast round hall was filled with light from a thousand blue-burning torches held high by servants in bright cerulean livery. Seated all around were the wizards, mostly dressed in indigo robes, but some in ultramarine and cobalt blue, depending on their rank. Each wore a small, turquoise cap with a navy tassle in the middle.

In their midst, seated alone, was a tall figure dressed in white. Her long blue-black hair was brushed out around her shoulders. Her arms and head were bare, and her skin was a glowing aquamarine colour.

As Fleabag looked down, the figure looked up and smiled, but said nothing.

Trembling, Kern peered over the edge of the balustrade. His knuckles and his face were quite white and he was sweating with fear. He stared wide-eyed at the cat.

'Umm,' Fleabag commented as he jumped down to sit beside the boy. 'We've found out what's happening.

It looks like trouble for the Ring Fire. Go and find your violin; we will need the strength of your music to give us courage. I'll fetch the others. Run as fast as you can; you needn't hide. They won't be after you. As I said, they've got other things to think about.'

Kern, still stooping low, slipped through the door at the far end of the balcony. Fleabag could hear his nervous steps running along the warren of hallways beyond.

The cat shivered as the gathered wizards began a slow chant. The sound made him feel cold. He sprang through the gap of the open door and ran back towards their rooms. As he rounded the last corner, he ran right into Gemma and Phelan, almost knocking them both over.

Fleabag did not waste time on apologies. 'Quick, come with me! Kern and I have found what is wrong. By the looks of it, the wizards are doing something to Rowanne!'

Gemma and Phelan followed Fleabag until the cat signalled a warning. The door creaked open, making the friends wince, but the noise was swallowed by the wizards' chanting, which had swollen from a soft sound in the choir to a full-throated anthem taken up by all present.

Everywhere was bitterly cold. Gemma and Phelan huddled together with Fleabag for warmth. The chill seemed to be sweeping through the air like a winter's gale. Yet this was a more sinister cold than a mere drop in temperature. It soaked into the skin of the listeners, beckoning them deeper and deeper into the blue, magical world, until there seemed no hope of ever again coming up to light and warmth…

The words of the wizards' cantor were clear and sharp as an icicle piercing the heart…

'There is no hope,
The great night has come,
the light has gone away.
There is no dawn…'

Gemma shuddered. The words were from the opening part of the Fire Festival ceremony! She nudged Phelan. How often they had sung that together. But surely the wizards wouldn't sing the next part, the proclamation of hope? What were *wizards* doing singing this, of all songs?

But the next verse *was* different:

'The night is ours
as surely as the day
has died for ever.
The night is ours
to work in as we will.

The night has come
when ice and fear will reign.
With Fire's death
at our command.'

Fleabag began to scratch at a wandering flea. 'What do you two think?'

Phelan shook his head. 'I don't believe it! She's gone over to the wizards! Goodness knows what secrets she'll tell them!'

'Not Rowanne!' Gemma went pale at the thought. 'She's no traitor!'

'But she *is*!' Phelan insisted. 'Use your eyes! She's about to be invested down there, and she's turned her back on the Ring Fire and everything.'

'But she told us that whatever we saw or heard, she would be doing it for the Ring Fire's sake!' Gemma replied. 'She may be unutterably stupid, but she would never betray us!'

Fleabag stretched his head over the balustrade. 'I think you'd better *see* what's happening down there,' he whispered.

The friends peered cautiously over the carved stone balcony, and watched Rowanne being dressed in a brilliant robe of shimmering blue light. It hurt their eyes to look at the scene. Rowanne did not look happy.

'See,' Gemma whispered again. 'She's not doing it for herself – she's suffering!'

Gemma's heart missed a beat as Rowanne looked up at them. She opened her mouth as if to say something... then shut it again.

Phelan and Gemma ducked and hid, hearts pounding in their mouths. Everyone would know they were there. As Fleabag would have said, if they were caught they would be dogmeat!

Just then the anthem came to an end, and a clear voice rang out: 'Do you, Princess Rowanne de Montiland, Arch Wizard of our order, accept the honour of the High Chancellorship of the Holy Order of All Wizards for as long as you live?'

There was a split second's hesitation, then Rowanne's deep, clear voice echoed around the hall, 'I do.'

'And do you swear to give your life's blood to promote and maintain the principles of the Holy Order of All Wizards, to keep the Blue Flame burning in the hearts of all who follow you?'

This time there was a definite uncomfortable pause. Rowanne stared around the hall filled with expectant faces, then up at her friends in the balcony. Her eyes were wide in what seemed to be panic. 'Help!' she mouthed.

Her friends looked down in horror. They could see she was terrified, but they could do nothing to help her.

'She wasn't expecting that one,' Fleabag commented. 'I'll bet my last three paws that whatever is happening down there is more than she ever bargained for.'

'Sssh!' Phelan warned, 'they're not finished with her yet!'

The clear voice of the questioner rang out again and repeated the question. Rowanne swayed a little and whispered, 'I do.'

'And do you swear on your life's blood to destroy utterly the enemies of the Blue Flame?' The questioner's voice spoke with a gloating thickness in it.

This time Rowanne looked terrified and said nothing. There was a long, deadly silence.

Gemma glanced at Phelan again. 'I don't honestly think she expected any of this. She just thought that the Blue Magic had to be stood up to, and being on the *inside* to do it put her in a stronger position than being on the outside. But they've trapped her. The wizards will never let her renege on these vows. She's either very brave or very foolish.'

'Perhaps she's both,' Phelan replied sadly. 'I also fear there's nothing we can do for her. We now know the truth. She has been very cynically and very carefully manoeuvred into position to become our enemy. She wanted to be our friend from within their camp, but it's all miserably backfired.'

The unbearable silence stretched on and on, until from below came a small strangled cry as a silver sword was pressed to Rowanne's throat.

Suddenly, from somewhere not far away, came the strains of a violin playing the anthem of the Ring Fire.

Fleabag bristled his fur and tail until he looked twice his size, then launched himself over the balcony. With a bloodcurdling caterwaul, he landed on the back of the neck of Rowanne's assailant, who fell to the floor, gore streaming from several long cuts that ran down his back. Though they were no deeper than a cat's claw, they made the man writhe and scream as his blood stained his blue robes a deep warm red.

Gemma knew what she must do. She did not have the courage to jump like Fleabag, but she held her arms open wide, letting the Ring Fire burn as she called out loud: 'Behold, the Fire Maiden and the Black Cat have returned!'

At the same moment, Phelan threw back his head and sang, in his rich, warm voice:

'Fire Giver,
In our darkest hour,
give us light.'

14

Rescuing Rowanne

Confusion broke out in the hall below. No one seemed interested in trying to capture Phelan and Gemma. The wizards didn't really know what had happened.

Fleabag's victim was rolling around on the floor, complaining that a whole army with knives had attacked him, and others were telling tales of blinding lights in the skies and terrible voices from the depths that had filled the hall at the moment of the new Chancellor's initiation. Some said this meant she would be the greatest Chancellor ever, and others that she would be the worst.

No one even knew for sure whether or not she had taken the final vow.

No one could think of what they were supposed to be doing. Wizards and servants were rushing this way and that, hopelessly blocking every passageway. For some reason, everyone was elbowing and pushing to be in the thickest part of the crowd where the pandemonium was greatest.

A hundred different arguments raged in every part of the hall. One or two of the senior wizards were arguing about whether the right spells had been used during the ceremony. 'Old M'Kinnik is past it!' exclaimed the tall, beautiful Vice Chancellor. 'I clearly heard him say '*Dominus*, not *Domina*. That's bound to mess up the ceremony if you have a female Chancellor! M'Kinnik is losing his marbles, if you ask me. He was just not concentrating... now if only they had let *me* do the initiation, I'd have...'

And a freckled young man with a mop of ginger hair was wildly gesticulating with his wand while he tried to explain how a wrong movement at the vital moment could have sent sparks across the ceiling and set some drapery alight somewhere, giving the appearance of lights in the air. But his listeners didn't care, for his wild wand-waving had turned them all into pale blue frogs. He ducked in alarm as the wizards' giant crow swooped down from her perch, high in the rafters, and began to pick the frogs up, one by one, for her supper.

At one end of the hall, the air was crackling with strange glowing patterns as wizards swooped their wands this way and that, analysing whether M'Kinnik had done a withyshins double extraloop with the left hand, as he should have done, or a dipped double sweep. The difference was slight, but vital. They didn't seem to care that they had burned their robes, and scorched the fine polished woodwork of the floor.

In another corner, a group of more academic wizards had summoned whole libraries of books which arrived unescorted, floating through the air like a flight of disorderly hornets, bashing and battering their way through the crowds. Anyone in the way of a stray volume was clouted around the ears by heavy tomes of disruptive spells and discourses on bad omens at inductions.

The resultant dizzy heads and concussed brains only added to the confusion; wizards sat or lay where they fell, nursing their heads and shoulders, and yelling for servants to fetch bowls of warm water to bathe the wounds, poultices for bruises and bandages for bleeding faces.

As the menials scurried away to do as they had been bidden, a whole detachment of the University guard, in their dark- and light-blue costume, came marching at double time down the long corridor, knocking the servants aside, and tangling their spears and swords in each other's legs. The more they became entangled, the faster they tried to march onwards, ploughing into an ever-increasing heap of angry comrades as they did so.

Soon everywhere was a mass of squirming, screaming and complaining bodies, lit by the pale-blue torch lights. No one could see clearly enough to work out how to get untangled, and no one was willing to give way to anyone else, so determined were they that their mission or errand was more important than anyone else's.

Within moments fighting broke out. Fists and swords and silver serving trays, even torches from the brackets on the walls, were pressed into service as impromptu weapons.

Phelan and Gemma did not wait to see the fun. They fled the balcony and managed to get back to their rooms without being challenged, without even a spell or a crow or a booby trap to stop them. The people of the University were so turned in on themselves, they seemed to have forgotten about the cat, the Fire Maiden and the singer: if they had ever really seen them in the first place!

Gemma did not feel like reminding them.

Down in the hall, Fleabag and Rowanne slipped through the angry crowd of shouting wizards. In their midst were a group of philosophical mages who were so busy arguing about whether Rowanne had or had not been inducted as Chancellor of All Wizards, that they did not notice her slipping between them, an indigo cloak pulled low over her face. Fleabag nudged her feet this way and that until he had manoeuvred her through a doorway which led to a deserted passageway beyond.

'Quick, in here!' he hissed. In the blink of an eye, Fleabag sped forwards, with Rowanne hard on his paws. The Princess opened her hand, and a small flame of blue light cast eerie shadows along the black shadowed corridors.

'Put that out!' Fleabag snapped crossly. 'I will *not* be led by the Blue Magic, and I can see perfectly well without it, anyway.'

'But *I* can't see a thing,' Rowanne whined as she closed her hand, extinguishing the baleful glow.

'Well, I can!' Fleabag retorted. 'You'll just have to trust me for the first time in your silly life!' he snapped.

'What do you mean, "silly"? You don't appreciate the dangers I have put myself through for you!' she replied angrily. 'I am a hero for the Ring Fire! I have risked everything to become a spy in the wizards' midst!'

'Rubbish!' Fleabag replied. 'I don't know what you thought you were doing, but it was far from heroic, and now you have got us all into terrible trouble!'

'Ouch!' Rowanne gasped as she stumbled into a wall.

'Sssh!' the cat ordered. 'Bend down and keep your hand on the tip of my tail. That's it. Don't grip it, it's very sensitive, you know!'

And within a few minutes, as they turned a corner, the soft strains of Kern's violin could be heard.

'Thank goodness, it's not far now,' Fleabag whispered. 'I was beginning to wonder if I had taken a wrong turning a little way back. Follow that sound!'

'I can't...' Rowanne gasped, letting go of Fleabag's tail and clapping her hands to her ears. 'It hurts! I can't bear to hear it! It makes me want to run away! Oh Fleabag, what's happened?'

'You've been extremely stupid! That's what!' the cat replied, as he pushed at a door with his front paws.

The door swung open, and a bright splash of golden light flooded the corridor with its glow.

Rowanne jumped back, yelping as if she had been burned. 'Help! I can't stand it!' she cried, shielding her eyes, yet still trying to block her ears at the same time.

Gemma stood in the doorway and held out her hands to her old friend. 'Come in. Have some food, and we'll talk about what is to be done.'

'But I can't...' Rowanne protested. 'It's the Ring Fire – it's burning me, I can't take it... and that music... it's like nails scratching down a chalk board... I'm frightened, Gemma. I wanted to help you, but now I find I can't stand you!'

'Well, come in, at least. No one's going to hurt you...'

'But I can't... I physically can't...' Rowanne wailed.

15

Banishing the Blue

Gemma and Phelan exchanged glances. They knew
what this meant: Rowanne had too much of the Blue
Magic in her to be able to stand the sight or the
sound of the Ring Fire!

Rowanne was no longer the tall, powerful woman
she had once been, but smaller and almost frail-
looking. She seemed to have aged at least twenty
years in the last few days.

'She can't have gone over to the Blue Magic altogether,' Gemma whispered to her friends. 'She's still
standing there, despite the fact that it's causing her
terrible pain to do so.'

'We can't leave her here all night,' Phelan whispered. 'The wizards will be after her blood. She didn't
make the final vow; they'll kill her if they find her.'

'I don't think so,' Fleabag answered. 'No one
knows what *really* happened. From what the wizards
were saying down there, it seems I acted so hero-
ically – at precisely the right moment (as usual) –
that they are totally confused. They believe the man
who was initiating Rowanne was attacked by an
army of knifemen. Gemma, holding the Ring Fire,

was a flash of lightning or something, and Phelan's singing was a voice from the deep. All good stuff, but at this precise moment, none of us is in danger – we're just not in the equation.'

At that moment, Kern came into the study, holding his violin. He saw Rowanne standing outside the door, and tried to run. Phelan grabbed his arm. 'Don't go, no one blames you for what you did. You were being bullied by M'Kinnik, and you didn't know any better.'

Kern stuttered something, and tried to hide.

'I won't betray you, boy,' Rowanne assured him. 'I may be the Chancellor, but believe it or not, I'm still on your side!' And with that she burst into tears and ran away. Gemma tried to follow her to bring her back.

'Please leave me alone!' Rowanne called out. 'The Ring Fire hurts too much!' Then, as she rounded a corner that took her out of sight, she called back, 'Get rid of everything that glows blue, Gemma. Anything a wizard has touched will betray you in the end!' And she was gone.

Sadly, Gemma returned to their study. 'Put the lights out. Rowanne says that anything that glows blue will betray us. I noticed that some of these books glowed blue in the dark; we'll put them outside first.'

'How can they betray us?' Kern asked.

'Who knows?' Phelan replied. 'Perhaps anything with even a smear of blue magic might carry a spell or may become the wizards' ears? Whatever it is, if it's that awful sickly blue colour, it's out as far as I'm concerned!'

When the candles were out, Gemma and Phelan pulled the books that glowed blue off the shelves and stacked them neatly outside the door. They took down a painting with strange symbols drawn around the frame. The rest of the room seemed to be quite ordinarily dark and peaceful. Phelan checked his bedroom and threw out a silver candlestick that had an eerie glow, and after that, Gemma could only see blueness around Kern's violin.

'That's the only thing that means anything to him in the whole world,' Gemma thought to herself. 'And he *is* playing the Ring Fire music on it. Perhaps that will make the blue go away.'

Gemma was torn. She knew Rowanne was right. But would the trouble it would cause Kern to take the fiddle from him prove worse than having a little Blue Magic in their midst? Perhaps a violin that the Chancellor of All Wizards had once touched might not be totally soaked with magic, just – well, smudged with it. Ordinary people left fingerprints wherever they touched, so perhaps it was the same with wizards – and equally harmless.

She relit the candles with Ring Fire to give the room extra protection, then she went outside the study door and did a strange thing: she ran her fingers all around the door posts, step and jamb, until the whole entryway was aglow with a thin thread of Ring Fire. Then she did the same at each window. The fire in the grate already glowed with the Ring Fire's ancient golden flames.

'We are safe now,' she said, as she sat down at the table with her friends. 'Play for us again, Kern, and then we must get some sleep. Tomorrow is the first trial.'

Kern bent over the King and shook him gently. 'Sire, the wizards have sent for you. It is almost time for the fight. Your breakfast has been brought up. I've checked it, and there is neither spell nor poison in it. Come, eat and wash or you'll never be ready in time.'

Phelan groaned as he stood. He was stiff all over from the strenuous hours in the practice yard the day before. In the study he sat on the settee and stroked Fleabag, who had already claimed most of the cushions as his own. 'How are the scratches on your back?' he asked.

The cat stretched gingerly and turned his neck to inspect the wounds. 'They look clean enough.' He licked at the scars. 'Hmm, they taste all right as well. Time will tell. Where is my breakfast?' and he jumped carefully onto the floor where Phelan had placed a fresh, chopped trout. 'Why *do* they insist on cutting my food up in this place?' he moaned. 'I'm not a kitten and when it's all in pieces I can't drag it around the floor and make the carpet smell all fishy!'

Phelan laughed. 'Perhaps that's precisely why they do it!'

Fleabag sniffed in disgust, picked up the fishhead and took it behind the coal scuttle to crunch in peace.

After breakfast, the sergeant at arms arrived to help Phelan put his armour on. Each part had been polished and oiled to perfection. When he was dressed, Phelan looked every inch a King, with his black curly beard poking out from under his visor, and the emblem of the Ring Fire resplendent on his breastplate.

Kern, who was to act as the King's squire, picked up Rowanne's sword and led the way to the tournament field where the trial was to take place.

A herald of the University escorted the royal party towards their own gold-coloured pavilion at the far end of the field. It was a cold, blustery day and, here and there, the snow from the day before had settled in powdery patches. The ground was hard as iron.

The refuge of the pavilion was most welcome. The King's men had lit a fire in a brazier and set out several camp chairs covered with thick fleeces. Apples were already roasting and ginger tea was brewing, giving off a heart-warming smell.

Fleabag jumped onto one of the chairs, and immediately curled up for a snooze. Gemma sat quietly in a corner to look into the Ring Fire, whilst Kern strapped the King's scabbard on for him. The boy seemed sullen and moody. Phelan tried to cheer him up. 'I know we will reach your mother soon,' he smiled. 'As soon as the trials are over and the wizards are defeated, there will be no more danger, and the Ring Fire will return her to us, I am sure.'

Kern said nothing, but shrugged.

Phelan rested his heavy, gauntleted hands on Kern's shoulders. 'We *will* win, somehow. Even if I'm killed today, all will be well in the end. The Ring Fire is stronger than the Blue Magic. I can promise you that.'

Kern turned his head away. He didn't want Phelan to sense the worry he felt. When he had gone to his attic to sleep, the stable lads were laughing at Phelan's sword skills. It was not that he was a bad fighter, but they all knew of Grimbold's reputation. He blushed and bit his lip. 'Can I make a suggestion, sire?' he asked at last.

Phelan smiled. 'Thank you. We need all the ideas we can get at the moment.'

The boy kicked his shoes nervously against a table leg. 'I really don't like magic, but I do know a few simple spells. Would you like me to use them? Just to protect you, of course.'

Phelan shook his head. 'It's kind of you, but we will not have anything to do with magic. The Ring Fire works with quietness and confidence in what is right. But if you really want to help, I should be grateful if you would hold my spare sword and give me water when I need it. Then you will have done me a great service. Now, the heralds are calling. It is time to go.'

16

The Trial of Strength

Grimbold stood a full head taller than Phelan. His armour was a light, fine chain mail covered with huge plates of blue iron. His helmet was topped with a nodding plume of azure feathers that swayed in the icy wind. The crowd that huddled under furs in the stands either side of the lists, were obviously great fans of his. He lifted his massive fists to their cheers as he strode into the centre of the arena.

Phelan stepped out of the golden tent and walked forward, trying hard to remember everything Rowanne had taught him. A few cheers came from his men at arms, and Gemma and Fleabag, of course. But his walk was a lonely one. He tried not to be daunted by the sight of Grimbold. He stood a chance if he kept his head…

He shivered as he surveyed his opponent. It might have been fear, but it seemed to him that the bitter cold seeped everywhere under his woollen shirt. Steel plate is not the best thing to wear on a freezing day. The icy cold hurt his hands as he tried to grip the pommel of Rowanne's sword firmly. He hoped desperately that he would warm up as the fight got under way.

Phelan didn't have long to think about his discomfort, for scarcely had he entered the arena before Grimbold lifted his sword high above his head and slammed the blade down. Phelan swayed to one side and the sharp edge narrowly missed his shoulder.

'Don't you salute your opponent?' Phelan shouted. 'Whatever happened to the rules of combat?'

'What rules?' came the gruff reply, accompanied by a long sideways slicing cut that caught Phelan on the greaves that covered his leg. The shock almost toppled him, but he managed to straighten himself. At least he had the measure of his opponent now. Long, wide sweeps and no manners.

Phelan used his smaller size and greater agility to dodge and duck Grimbold's moves. He hoped the giant would tire before he did. But his tactics seemed to make the stranger angry. Quite suddenly the giant abandoned the long, wide manoeuvres and returned to the heavy, downward cuts aimed at Phelan's arms. Grimbold's sword was impossibly long – it was almost as long as himself, and as wide as a man's forearm. Phelan stared in wonder at the great iron blade as time after time it came thundering against him. He could not take his eye from it; he was amazed that anyone could even *lift* such a weapon. It took all his concentration, and although he defended himself well, he could not plan an attack.

As the end of the bout was called, Kern came running to him with a drink. Fleabag came out onto the field and clambered onto Phelan's slippery metal lap. 'Each blow he is giving you is a point – you realize that, don't you? He's scored eleven so far, and you have only two. Try to at least touch him, score points, do some attacking! Stop dancing around like a jelly!'

Phelan shook his head. 'But have you seen the length of his sword? I can't get near the man. He handles it like it a threshing machine. Anything within range would be totally demolished within seconds!'

'Well, at least try to score some points, so if you're going to lose, you won't do it so miserably!' Fleabag cajoled. Just then the trumpet sounded for the combatants to come together again.

Phelan groaned and got to his feet. But scarcely had he moved forward, when Grimbold pushed his left foot forward and swung his sword in low under Phelan's guard, unbalancing him in a single movement. The crowd went wild with joy as the young King fell hard onto the icy ground.

'I *knew* there was something Rowanne told me I had to remember,' he muttered to himself, as the marshal of the lists proclaimed Grimbold the winner.

Back in the tent, Kern played music softly on his violin as Phelan tugged the armour off. He accepted his sergeant at arms' offer of help, and drank from a horn of hot, spiced mead that Gemma gave him. He was bruised and his pride was injured, but no further damage had been sustained. Gemma put ointment on the bruises and made him lie down and rest.

'The race doesn't begin for an hour,' she told him. 'At least try to relax. Do you want Kern to keep playing?'

'Oh yes, please,' he murmured as he drifted off to sleep. 'It makes it seem as if everything's going to be all right.'

Just before noon, Phelan roused himself and washed. This time he felt more confident as he splashed his face with water, and pulled on a light linen shirt and shorts.

'I've walked the track,' Fleabag told him. 'I can't see or smell any sign of booby traps. That doesn't mean there aren't any, of course. The ground is still as hard as stone, but the wind will be at your back for the home stretch. Your opponent is a lad from the south, like yourself. He looks rather like a human greyhound.'

'Thanks,' Phelan replied. 'I really needed to know that.' And he began his warm-up exercises.

The noon-day trumpet sounded and Phelan walked out onto the track that had been marked around the perimeter of the lists: three times around and one last home sprint up the middle. It was enough to get his teeth into, but not enough to tire him. He grinned. This time he felt much more confident, and he did not mind the lack of cheers. *This* was something he could do.

As he crouched over the starting line, he glanced at his opponent. He was a lean dark-skinned man, about his own age. As Fleabag had said, he was the nearest thing to a human greyhound. What would be his weakness? The bends or the straights?

At last a bugle sounded the start, and Phelan felt the cold air fill his lungs with an exhilaration he hadn't felt in a long time. He was running, and that, to him was like flying. It gave him such a wonderful sense of freedom and joy, it always made him want to sing. But he daren't let himself; he had to keep every last breath for the race. Instead he sang in his head.

As his feet hit the cold earth rhythmically, he found he was making up words that celebrated the wonderful feeling of being alive. The sky was blue – but a healthy natural blue, not a sickly magical colour. And the freshness of the air made him feel buoyant. At the edge of the field, the town of Porthwain, with its crumbling, elegant buildings, looked very beautiful. But Phelan did not let himself become distracted. He had to think about running.

Thud, thud, thud, his feet hit the hard ground. Where was his opponent? Phelan glanced around. They were about neck and neck. The other runner had the advantage of the bend, but Phelan let him take it. The wind was against them for this short stretch and he wanted to slide into the other man's wake. It would give him a rest, ready for the much-needed push ahead.

To his surprise, Phelan noticed the marshall's flag was up for the last lap. Had they really been around twice already? He must really concentrate; he would not have been so relaxed had he realized the race was almost over. There was virtually no time left to pull forward, and the other man was already surging ahead. He would just give himself a few more strides of taking it easy, then, as they came around the next bend into the straight, he would push ahead... But he had to time it just right.

At that second, Phelan caught the edge of his foot against a stone and stumbled. He cried out as pain shot through his ankle. His opponent turned at the sound, but did not slacken. Instead he lowered his head and grinned as he sensed that the race could be his. Phelan tried to get his stride going again, but his

125

ankle hurt too much. The other runner was a long way in front, and Phelan's heart sank. He was at least the equal of the wizard's champion. He should at least have managed a tie, but he had lost it all now. But he would keep going. There was no honour in just giving up.

Then suddenly Phelan heard something – the strains of Kern's violin, playing a stirring melody from the Fire Festival. It revived his spirit and made him sprint, forgetting his twisted ankle. He had to run with the music.

The tempo quickened, and Phelan quickened too.

Soon he was level with the greyhound-man, then, just as the blue ribbon was pulled tightly across their path, Phelan found the pain in his ankle didn't matter. He was singing and running all at the same time. His lungs felt as if they could hold all the air in the world. He had enough breath for everything! He sang and ran and ran and sang.

The other runner stared in horror and disbelief as Phelan snapped the ribbon only a few hand-spans ahead of him! Phelan shouted in triumph, and Gemma and Fleabag danced with joy around their victorious friend. Inside the tent, Kern put down his violin and sat exhausted on a chair. He had never played like that in his life. He really didn't know how he had found it in himself, or why he had chosen that tune. It had just seemed important at the time.

In her place in the seat of honour, the Chancellor of All Wizards, the Princess Rowanne de Montiland smiled as she lifted a hand to silence the angry crowd.

'The first trial is a draw. One all!' she announced. 'We will resume with the next trial tomorrow at noon, when the cat Fleabag will meet with our noble sister Heithra in a battle of wit and wisdom.'

And with that she bowed to the crowds and left.

17

Good Enough

Phelan fell asleep as soon as he reached his room. His body ached, and he was heavy-hearted as well. Although he had won the race, he was unhappy that he had lost the sword fight. He had known he stood little chance of beating Grimbold, but secretly he had hoped that maybe the Ring Fire would help him win.

He slept heavily, hoping to blot out all thought of the next day – the trial of wit and wisdom. Fleabag was surely the sharpest wit amongst them all, but against learned academics who were capable of reading and learning a book just by holding it... redoubtable cat that he was, did even Sir Fleabag Scrag-Belly stand a chance?

Fleabag and Gemma spent the afternoon trying to remember riddles and work out cunning word plays. They wanted to find something that might just catch out an over-confident wizard. But they weren't optimistic. Everything depended on understanding the way the wizards thought – and neither of them stood a chance of fathoming *that!* 'If only we knew a friendly wizard!' Gemma sighed as she screwed up yet another sheet of paper and threw it across the room, missing the bin entirely.

Just then someone knocked timidly on the door.

Gemma opened it and sighed. Rowanne was standing outside smiling coyly. 'I wasn't eavesdropping, honestly, but I couldn't help overhearing what you were saying. I'd love to help, and I really can!'

Gemma stepped back. 'Would you like to come in?' she asked as cordially as she could, although she didn't really want any interruptions.

Rowanne shook her head. 'No, thank you – your rooms are a little full of the Ring Fire for my comfort. It's not that I don't love it any more, I do. It just... hurts. But I do need to talk to you. I can be that friendly wizard you need. That's what I went through all this *for*, after all! If only you'd let me, there's so much I could help you with.'

As she spoke, Rowanne looked so much like the faithful friend they knew and loved – yet so changed at the same time.

Gemma swallowed hard. 'I don't want to hurt your feelings, but we cannot accept your help. Surely you can see that?'

Rowanne looked deeply disappointed. 'I wish I hadn't bothered to go to all this trouble for the Ring Fire. I always used to feel that nothing I did was good enough for it. Now I've tried extra hard to do something special, and it's only made things worse.'

Gemma wanted to throw her arms around Rowanne and hug her, but the sight of her old friend's eerily glowing skin held her back. Instead she just spread her hands wide and looked Rowanne in the eye. 'Perhaps you've been trying *too* hard? Why don't you dump all this silly Blue Magic nonsense? You don't have to be "good enough" for the Ring Fire, you just have to be *you*! You're still loved and wanted, and there's always enough forgiveness for whatever anyone has done.'

'You don't understand, do you?' Rowanne said bitterly as she turned to go.

Gemma caught hold of the wizard's cloak, which burned her hand with its icy coldness. 'Listen, I'd love to talk with you, but only as Rowanne, not as the Chancellor of All Wizards. If you can't come into our rooms, we'll go somewhere neutral. Is there somewhere in town we could meet?'

Rowanne turned back with obvious relief in her face. 'I daren't go far,' she whispered. 'If *they* think we're going away from the wizards' part of the University, they'll suspect me of being up to something. I've got to be careful. I'll make it known that I'm going to try to muddle your minds with spells of confusion under a pretence of chatting to you. Come to the library, it's very public there, so everyone can see we're meeting, but we'll sit where we can't be overheard easily. Be there in an hour.'

And with that she turned and walked away. Gemma was relieved Rowanne didn't float this time. She shut the door with a sigh and looked at her friends.

'Well?' Fleabag asked, 'are we going?'

Gemma nodded sadly. 'I am, certainly. I miss Rowanne, and if I can do anything to help her, I will.'

'It might be a trap,' suggested Phelan. 'I trust the real Rowanne, but is that really her?'

'Let's go and find out,' Fleabag proposed.

At the appointed time, the friends walked down to the library. They had not invited Kern to join them.

It seemed best that he spent as much time as possible about his old duties as kitchen boy and stablehand so as not to arouse suspicion about too many dealings with the party from Harflorum. If people did not suspect him, he was safe. The wizards might not be able to hurt Claire, but Kern's life could be in great danger.

The late afternoon sun streamed through the library windows, sending golden shafts of light across the leather-bound books, gleaming on the azure silk ribbons that held the ancient, crumbling volumes together.

Seated in a small study area at the far end of the long room was Rowanne, dressed in the simple blue robes of an ordinary wizard. Her dark indigo hair was tied back and, apart from the strange glow from her skin, she looked almost her old self. The friends pulled up chairs near to her and she began to speak very quickly and quietly. She handed Gemma a plain white envelope. 'Here are the riddles and questions that Fleabag will be asked tomorrow. Take it, and burn it when you have read it.'

Fleabag and Gemma exchanged glances. The cat shook his head, and Gemma pushed the envelope away. 'We can't. That would be cheating. And anyway, it may be a trap.'

Rowanne looked offended. 'Honestly, Gemma! *Would* I?'

Phelan smiled. 'I don't think Gemma means that *you* would trap us, but the wizards may be testing *your* loyalty. If Fleabag miraculously knows the answers tomorrow, they will have a pretty good idea who told us. Then it would be curtains for you. Who knows whether these books, even these chairs and desks, have listening spells cast by the wizards? They could know exactly what we are saying, every second. You said yourself that anything that is wizard-blue will ultimately betray us.'

Rowanne glowered. 'But don't you think that *I* would know? I *am* the Chancellor after all!'

'We had noticed!' Fleabag sniffed disapprovingly. 'Thanks, but no thanks. We have decided on the questions we are going to ask, and we will have to take what comes from the wizards.'

Rowanne did not look pleased as she pushed the long envelope back into a pocket in her robes. 'As you wish,' she sniffed. 'But what about the day after? The trial of magic. I had, as you know, planned to take this trial for you. But, well, due to unforeseen circumstances, I won't be able to. I knew I was being inducted as an arch wizard the other night, but not that I would become the Chancellor. This means I cannot be seen to act on your behalf.'

Fleabag bristled his whiskers and frowned.

'Honestly!' Rowanne went on. 'I really *didn't* know.'

'Leave it, Fleabag,' Phelan frowned. 'Whether she knew or not is immaterial. The question is, Gemma, do you feel that *you* should be taking the trial on behalf of the Ring Fire?'

Gemma closed her hands under the table, and felt the warming, soothing trickle of golden light between her fingers. It was safe, it was calm, and it told her very clearly to do nothing.

'No,' she said definitely. 'I will not be taking the trial.'

Rowanne blanched. 'Will you let me summon a

wraith to appear in your likeness and take your place?'

Fleabag leaped onto the table and hissed angrily at Rowanne. Phelan thumped the table with his fist. '*NO!*' he shouted loudly, so everyone in the library turned to listen. 'The Ring Fire will fight its own battles its own way. It does not need the help of wraiths and wizards!'

By now, Phelan was leaning across the table and quite red in the face. A small crowd of shocked wizards had gathered nearby, eager to catch the fun of the row. But Fleabag bristled his fur and yowled at them in a way that made them all turn and run. Their fear of him had not evaporated, and Fleabag hoped it never would.

Gemma stood, and said in a gentler tone of voice: 'Listen, Rowanne, whatever reasons you had for becoming a wizard, they were wrong. Whatever reasons you had for accepting the trials on our behalf, they were wrong too. Now, either renounce the Blue Magic and help us as a friend of the Ring Fire, or leave us alone.'

And with that, Gemma turned and walked from the library, followed closely by Phelan and Fleabag, stepping as proudly as a three-legged cat can, hissing and flashing his fire-golden eyes this way and that.

As the cat walked by, the wizards glowered, but did not dare cast a single spell.

18

Wit and Wisdom

At noon precisely Fleabag sat on a golden-red velvet
cushion on an ornate chair in the middle of the
Great Hall, the very room where he, Gemma and
Phelan had defeated the old Chancellor. The
memory of that day gave the cat confidence, despite
the sea of threatening faces and gowns of various
hues of blue that washed around him.

Fleabag faced his opponent, a thin, sour-faced
woman in an indigo gown. She leaned on the highly
polished table between them, put her skeletal fingertips together, and peered over them at Fleabag. She
did not seem to be the least bit daunted by the feline
nature of her opponent.

On the contrary, she looked more as if she was
contemplating a rather succulent-sounding menu,
and about to order the lot!

So this was Rowanne's 'noble sister' Heithra.

Fleabag looked a great deal calmer than he felt.
He had spent all morning with Gemma, peering into
the flame of the Ring Fire in the Fire Wielder's
hands. The comforting warmth had spread though
his three legs, right out to his ear-tips and his

whiskers. But even though Gemma had promised to keep him surrounded by the safety of the Fire while he went through his ordeal, he was now shivering inside. He hoped it did not show, but he could not help the tip of his tail twitching as he caught sight of Rowanne, coming to sit on one of the judges' seats on the dais at the top end of the hall.

M'Kinnik rose to his feet and read from a scroll. 'Each contestant will challenge the other with feats of wisdom and wit, strictly taking turns, until one contestant fails to answer. The trial will then have been won by whoever has answered the greatest number of questions correctly.'

At the sound of a small silver gong being struck, both Heithra and Fleabag stood and bowed formally to each other, although neither contestant took their eyes from each other's faces for a split second.

'Pray, go first,' Heithra said, in a voice that sounded like dry paper being screwed up.

Fleabag coughed slightly and stroked his whiskers with his paw. Here went nothing!

'My first is nobility, my second jumps high,
my third carries all, whatever I buy.
My fourth belies my expensive taste,
and my fifth and my last lies under my waist.

'Who am I?'

Fleabag swallowed hard. It was an easy one, obvious even, but he had to test the water somehow. So much depended on *how* this woman thought.

Heithra scarcely paused to take breath. '*Sir* is a

135

title of nobility, but I'm sure I can't see why you should be so honoured, just because you wear a golden earring. *Fleas* jump high, *bags* carry everything in them, *scrag* is the cheap cut of the meat – and more than a cat deserves – and your disgustingly fat *belly* lies under your waist, or it would if you had one. You are Sir Fleabag Scrag-Belly, although I strongly suspect that is not your real name.'

'You bet!' Fleabag muttered under his breath. Phelan was the only other living person who knew what his real name was. The cat had always kept it a closely guarded secret; it was his protection against the Blue Magic because no major spells could be cast without the victim's real name being used.

'*Please* try to stretch my brain at least a little, or I shall become bored very quickly,' Heithra went on. 'At least I can see this so-called challenge will be very short, if that is the best you can do.'

Fleabag blushed under his black fur and bristled his eye-brow whiskers angrily. But he could not deny she had got the answer correct. Now it was her turn. He listened intently.

'I'd better make it easy for you, poor puss,' Heithra sneered. 'I went out, and stood on a road with another road under me, a road above me, and a road on either side of me. Where was I?' Heithra put her head on one side and smiled, a chilling smile, showing neat, over-white teeth.

Fleabag took a deep breath. This was a different sort of riddle from the ones he had been rehearsing with Gemma. He had to stay calm and use his imagination. She was standing outside on a road, that was a good start. With another road under her, she could

136

be on a bridge over a stream, for that would be a road to a fish… then what could be the roads above and on either side? Fleabag closed his eyes and imagined standing on a road going over a bridge with something passing by on either side… That was it – *birds*! The air was their road, and that was all around! Joyfully he blurted out the answer.

He could see Heithra was annoyed, but he grinned gleefully under his whiskers. Perhaps he stood a chance after all! In his mind he threw away all the rhyming riddles he had learned. These were easier. All he had to do was think of something and find a difficult or obscure way of saying something – and he was good at being difficult!

'Who is armour-plated in silver mail, jumps higher than an athlete and goes away to come home?' he asked.

Again Heithra did not pause. 'A salmon,' she replied. 'They have silver scales and leap up waterfalls. They also leave their home rivers to grow up in far-off waters before recrossing wide oceans to come home to spawn. Now it's your turn. What was the drink I had yesterday? It was neither wine nor water, milk nor ale. It came in neither a stream nor a cup, yet only a humble person could drink it.'

'Well, that counts you out!' retorted Fleabag as his mind raced. How could anyone drink using neither a cup nor a stream? Only a humble person would drink whilst on his knees, so it was something to do with licking or lapping from something down low near the ground. That was easy, being a cat he did that all the time. Puddles? No. That would count as water and they always tasted unspeakable. *Dogs* drank from puddles. What would he drink from that was low down? 'Dew!' he shouted out loud.

It was a bit of a stretch of the imagination. Dew was a sort of water really... He glanced at Heithra's face. He needn't have worried. Two red spots of angry colour on her cheeks told him he was right!

'What has eight feet, four eyes and carries its knees above its head?' Fleabag asked quickly. He felt as if he was beginning to enjoy this!

'A spider,' Heithra replied, just as quickly. Then she cracked her knuckles before putting her finger tips together and peering over them again. 'What flies higher than an eagle, whistles like the wind, stings like a hornet and is hard to catch until it catches you?'

Fleabag closed his eyes and tried to imagine watching something flying very high, whistling, stinging, and so swift even Rowanne could not grasp it as it passed, yet out to catch *him*? The thought of Rowanne gave him the clue he needed. For he pictured her as she used to be, with the other knights in the practice yards, swinging their swords at dummies and shooting their long yew bows at the butts... 'An arrow!' he said triumphantly.

He was ready with the next one, for it followed on easily from the last: 'Who is the great protectoress dressed in bright colours who goes out for the day on a man's arm, yet comes home with blood on her bent back?' (Or it could go out on a woman's arm he thought, glancing across to Rowanne, who he could see had caught his drift easily.)

Heithra hesitated a second on this one. The idea of a great protectoress who was gaily dressed on a man's arm had thrown her for a moment or two. 'A shield!' she replied at last. 'It goes out on a man's arm, painted with bright heraldry, but by the end of the day's battle, its curved surface is covered with blood. Now,' she said, 'what is the great devourer who consumes the sea and hills, yet has no teeth? It fears the sun but scorns the power of men and women.'

Fleabag grinned. Gemma had taught him a rhyming version of this one! He had planned to use it himself. 'Fog!' he answered.

But then he panicked. All the riddles he had stored seemed suddenly to have fled his fish-filled brain. He had to think quickly – something – anything just to keep going... 'Four went out walking together, four hung around, staring at the ground. Two found the way ahead, two shooed off the dogs and a long, thin dirty one swung behind them all.'

Heithra shrugged contempuously. 'A cow. Four legs to walk with, four teats on her udder, two eyes, two horns and a dirty tail.' Then with a glance at the judges she added, 'unless you are going to make at least *some* attempt to tax my brain, I am going to ask one of the kitchen staff to take my place. This really is becoming very tedious.'

Fleabag stared very hard back. 'Well, you can't be so very clever yourself! I'm only a mere cat and you haven't caught me out yet, have you?'

Heithra flushed very red at the insult and rose to her feet. From her thin heights she stared down at Fleabag and hissed: 'Who is the traitor in your midst, and how should she be punished?'

Fleabag almost fell backwards off his cushion. He

felt himself go pale under his matted, black fur. He glanced quickly over his shoulder at Gemma, who looked equally stunned. Then from the corner of his eye he saw Phelan lean forward and shake his head.

Fleabag could sense Rowanne's fear from where she sat, although he did not risk looking at her. The cat knew what Phelan was trying to say: one betrayal never deserves another.

Fleabag had to risk losing the entire Challenge. He would have to trust the Ring Fire to think of something. He could only answer this one honestly. Even though he knew the answers to both questions, there was only one possible reply, and he gave it. 'It is not for me to say.'

The wizards cheered and clapped loudly and long. Heithra was lifted out of her seat and carried shoulder high around the hall. Fleabag turned to slink out of the room as quietly and inconspicuously as possible, but as he jumped down from the cushion, a loud, stentorian voice rang across the jubilant hubbub.

'*SILENCE*!'

Everyone stopped and turned to the figure of the High Chancellor, standing on her dais, her arms flung wide, and her too-blue eyes blazing in fury. Heithra was gently allowed to stand again.

'The cat has one more question!' Rowanne commanded. 'The trial is won by the person – or cat – who answers the most questions. Is that not right, M'Kinnik?'

The elderly wizard nodded, but looked confused. 'It is, my Lady, but what is your point?'

'My point is, that Heithra asked *two* questions last

140

turn, which means that she has asked six, and the cat, although he opened the trial, has only asked five.'

M'Kinnik shrugged. 'So what? That was two questions he couldn't answer, so he has doubly lost!' The crowd laughed at this, but Fleabag jumped back onto his cushion. If Rowanne was trying to get him a second chance, he would have to think very quickly. If the riddles they had begun with were wit, and Heithra's last two questions were wisdom, then he was also entitled to ask a question of wisdom. What should it be? He had no time to confer with the others. He would have to have something ready in case Rowanne won him a chance... Fleabag looked across at Gemma who was holding the Ring Fire in her open palm. The question he needed was in there somewhere...

Rowanne wasn't going to be put off by M'Kinnik. 'My point, my Lord,' she persisted, 'is that the cat should not have been asked two questions *together*. Heithra broke the rules that you yourself read out. You stipulated that the contestants were to take strict turns! She cheated, and therefore for that reason alone, the cat deserves one last question.'

Heithra shrugged as she strode back to her place. 'It makes absolutely no difference to me, my Lord M'Kinnik. I did not intentionally cheat. I was, I freely admit, a little carried away. I am quite happy to let the cat have another question if this makes my Lady, the High Chancellor of All Wizards, happy. The cat's questions are so inferior, that there will really not be a problem. Let him ask whatever he likes.' And she smiled magnanimously at Fleabag as she settled herself down, and once again peered disconcertingly over her thin fingertips.

Fleabag managed to focus beyond her, at the small glow of Ring Fire between Gemma's fingers.

And without thinking, he opened his mouth and asked, 'Where is the Ring's End?'

19

Another Riddle

Heithra went very pale and dropped her pointed fingers to the table. 'No one knows that! That is not a fair question!' She looked pleadingly towards the dais.

Rowanne spoke briefly with M'Kinnik and the third judge, an elderly man on her left. Then she waved her hand dismissively. 'You have trapped yourself out of your own mouth, Heithra. You said, before all witnesses that the cat could ask any question he liked.'

Then M'Kinnik turned to Rowanne and hissed angrily, 'I told you she'd foul it up. *I'd* have done a far better job, if only you had listened to me!'

Rowanne said nothing, but rose from her seat. 'I declare this trial a draw,' she said, and turned and walked out.

No one moved or spoke. At last M'Kinnik stood and very slowly followed Rowanne. As he reached the door, he spoke quietly to a guard, and walked out.

The crowd broke into a noisy hubbub of dispute.

But as Gemma, Phelan and Fleabag tried to slip

away, the guards barred their way with business-like spears and swords. 'You ain't goin' anywhere,' a mean-looking man informed them. 'You're all under arrest. M'Kinnik's orders.'

'Arrest', thankfully, meant house arrest, in their rooms rather than in a dungeon. Fleabag was irritated not to be allowed out onto the tiles to think, but he soon found the wide window-ledge reasonably comfortable. Only Gemma was cross, because it meant opening the window every time he wanted to come in or out – which was frequently – and the winter air was very cold.

Phelan asked if Kern would be allowed to come and play his violin to them, and a generous bribe to the guard on duty ensured that the lad was not long in coming.

The boy played softly all afternoon, folk tunes, ballads, and wistful airs. Phelan, Gemma and Fleabag (when he eventually came inside to settle) sat quietly around the log fire, listening to the soothing tones of the boy's playing. No one spoke for a long time.

At last Fleabag broke the silence. 'Well, Gemma, where *is* the Ring's End, and what is it?'

'That's two questions! You're only allowed one!' Gemma laughed. Then she looked serious again. 'I don't know. In fact, I don't have the foggiest.' She looked questioningly at Phelan. His parents had once been servants of the Ring Fire in Rowanne's city of Erbwenneth. When they had been wrongfully put to death, he had lived with a wise man called Aelforth. All of these good people had told him stories and wisdom of the Ring Fire, long before he could understand what any of it meant.

Phelan looked at the heavy grey sky outside. 'I think it's something to do with where the Fire Giver is to be found:

> "If the Fire Giver you truly seek
> follow no track, green or bleak.
> Listen to the words I say:
> To the Ring's End make your way."'

'But what does that mean?' Gemma asked. 'It's like one of those riddles Fleabag and I were working on; a ring doesn't have an end!'

'It must mean something,' Fleabag argued. 'I'd not heard that rhyme before, yet I knew the question I had to ask just by looking into the Ring Fire in Gemma's hands. I don't know,' he sighed. 'I'm going to sleep. My head hurts, and not being able to run over the tiles for a snack to keep me going before teatime is really sapping my will to live.'

And with that he stretched out on the hearthrug and began to purr.

'How can he be so contented at a time like this!' Gemma grumbled affectionately. And she stroked his black, barrel-like tummy with the toe of her slipper. A few fleas jumped off, but Gemma brushed them away before they could nibble at her ankles.

Suddenly Kern stopped playing his violin. 'Do you mind if I make a suggestion? I know I'm not one of your Ring Fire people, but I've got an idea that might help.'

Phelan smiled and moved over so Kern could sit by the fire. 'It's not a matter of being "one of us" or not. I don't even know what that means. But you're our friend, and that's what matters. So give it a whirl, what's your idea?'

Kern twiddled his violin between his fingers and watched the firelight reflecting on its varnish. 'It's just that… Oh no, it sounds silly, and I don't know anything of your stuff. Sorry,' and he got up to play again.

'No, go on,' urged Gemma. 'Please. Even if it isn't the answer, it might give us a clue.'

Kern took a deep breath. 'Do you remember when I found my mother asleep in the strange fire, and you told me it wasn't magic, but it was real, and the Ring Fire had her, and she was safe?'

'Yes? Go on,' Phelan urged.

'And you said that the room could be wherever the Fire Giver wanted it to be?'

'Yes…?' Even Fleabag had woken up again.

'Well, it's just that, well, it seems to me that if that is so, then perhaps this Ring's End is somewhere near there. Because if that's the Fire Giver's room, then he or she might be there.' And Kern slumped back against the settee's cushions and waited for the laughter.

But none came. Instead Phelan slapped him on the back. 'Well done. You're quite right. It's obvious!'

'I've always felt that the Ring Fire could exist anywhere, even here,' Gemma added. 'And when you think about it, that would explain why you can't follow a "track" to get to it.'

Fleabag opened one golden eye. 'Of *course* he's right. *I* knew it all along, I just didn't want to embarrass you pathetic humans by my wit and wisdom. I knew you'd get there by and by. I was just testing to see how long it would take you to get the answer!' And with that, the incorrigible cat rolled over to toast his other side by the fire. In the wink of an eye he seemed to be asleep once more.

'It's all very well,' Gemma said thoughtfully, 'but *how* are we going to find that room again? We're under arrest, after all. We can't leave here without an escort.'

Kern bit his lip. 'I know you don't like magic and stuff, but I might be able to help there. I've known for a long time, I can do all sorts of things with my violin...'

'Well now you've got rid of that dreadful cat-gut you might be able to,' said Fleabag, although he was supposed to be asleep.

'Yes, well, sorry about that. But I can do things like put people to sleep, and wake them up, and I can make them feel happy or sad or anything really. But it's not magic, or at least I don't think it is. It's just something I can do, and I use it to help people, when they're tired or upset or sad. Never to harm them.'

'So what's your suggestion?' Phelan asked. 'If you're not using spells or potions, but it's just a natural talent you have, then I'm happy to hear what you have to say.'

'I agree,' said Gemma. 'I can't see anything wrong in soothing people's worries or making people want to dance.'

'Well,' Kern went on, plucking up courage, 'I know this building like the back of my hand. If you come with me, I might be able to lead you past guards, either with stealth, or with a little musical help to put the soldiers to sleep. And between us, we can spend the night searching for this secret room. I must admit, I want to find my mother again. I do believe what you say about her being safe and well, but I would like to see her for myself.'

'Of course you do. I'd feel the same – if I had a mother.' Gemma felt sad for a moment. She could not remember anything about her parents, and often wished she could. 'What do you think, Phelan? Are you happy with Kern's plan?'

Phelan nodded. 'Yes, I think we ought to try. If we can find the Ring's End, then we will be able to ask the Fire Giver what to do tomorrow. That is...' he hesitated, 'if you still don't think it's right to take the magical trial yourself, Gemma?'

'Certainly not!' she replied emphatically. 'I'm more certain than ever that the Fire Giver will sort this out in a way we haven't even thought of. But we do need help, and that room was a very special place. I'm certain I would feel stronger and more confident just by sitting there. Do you think that would be all right, Phelan?'

'Definitely!' he grinned. 'But Kern, if you can put people to sleep just by playing to them, how are *we* going to stay awake?'

Kern laughed and reached over to a candle softened by the heat of the fire. He pulled off a thick chunk of creamy-white wax. 'It's easy. Ear-plugs! I don't need them. I can play without affecting myself – unless I want to, that is. I'll lead you by touch and hand signals.'

20

Secret Ways

No amount of persuasion would entice Fleabag to wear ear-plugs. So, in the end, Gemma told him that if he fell asleep on the job she would leave him next to the nearest door and pretend he was a draught excluder. She was *not* going to carry him around for the whole evening.

Fleabag sniffily replied that he *never* fell asleep at inappropriate moments, least of all on the job, but his comments were only met with derisive laughter. So to test whether he could withstand Kern's music (and to be sure the ear-plugs worked), Kern played one of his best melodies for producing sleep.

Fleabag sternly sat to attention the whole time, and stared straight ahead, with his eyes as wide and golden as carriage-lamps. His eyelids did not flicker once. 'You see?' he said when Kern had finished, and the others had unblocked their ears. 'I'm perfectly in control of myself. I succumb to nothing!'

'Except to mouldy fish heads!' Gemma laughed, producing one from behind a cushion. 'How long has *that* been there, you miserable creature?'

'Ah!' Fleabag purred contentedly. 'I've been looking

for that. Give it here!' and he jumped up, snatched it from between Gemma's fingers, and took it off into a corner to give it his full and undivided attention.

That evening, when supper had been served and cleared away, Gemma contrived to open the study door a crack, without the guard challenging her. Once the wax earplugs were all in place, Kern lifted his violin and began to play. This time Fleabag's head nodded, and even Gemma and Phelan found their minds drifting as soft strains seeped though the candlewax plugs.

After a little while, Kern eased the door a little wider with his foot. There was still no challenge. Kern nodded to Fleabag who slipped outside to the dark, shadowy corridor. He disappeared with a whisk of his bottlebrush tail. Gemma followed, and Phelan came last, carrying Rowanne's sword strapped around his waist. He didn't want to use it, but took it along, just in case.

Phelan closed the door, in case anyone should be suspicious. With any luck, the sleeping guards, who were leaning against the wall, snoring nicely, would waken in a few moments and think they had just dozed off and no harm had been done.

Kern led them swiftly to the right, then up a steep spiral staircase. Up and up they went, seemingly for ever. At first the treads and banisters were made of ornately wrought patterns but, as it twisted nearer and nearer to the servants' quarters, the treads became narrow wooden boards with a plain iron rail.

At last, the friends found themselves breathless in a hexagonal room at the top of a tall tower, with views far across the plains beyond the town.

The moon was full. In its light, Gemma could see in the distance the mountains where she lived. How she wished she could be back there at her tiny cottage in the rocks with her two cats (talking grand-kittens of Fleabag's) and her garden. There was peace and quiet, time to listen to the Ring Fire and, best of all, no magic – blue or otherwise.

She sighed. But this had to be dealt with first. In the soft moonlight, Gemma could see that Kern looked disappointed. 'I had hoped that as this room is so nearly round, we might find the stone fireplace and my mother here. But I can see that it is not going to be as easy as that. At least here we can talk and think without being overheard.'

'Just a moment,' Fleabag warned. 'I had what I thought was a private chat in a place like this once, and I found one of Chancellor Domnall's crows was sitting on the roof, listening to every word.' The cat jumped up on the windowsill and craned his neck to look out. 'There's too much of an overhang; I can't really see.'

'I know,' Kern volunteered. 'I'll play one of my sleeping melodies.'

'At least if anyone is up there they can be sure of dropping off that way!' laughed Fleabag.

Phelan, Gemma and Kern looked most disapprov-ingly at the cat, but none of them could resist laughing at his awful joke. They all needed to laugh to ease the fear they were all feeling. Then they put their ear-plugs in, and Kern played.

After the tune was finished, Kern nodded, and the two other humans cleared their ears. Fleabag, how-ever, had to be woken up. He protested he had his eyes closed because he was trying to hear what he thought was a spying mouse. But no one believed him because he had been snoring so loudly.

'Now,' Phelan began, 'we are here to try to find the circular room with the stone fireplace. Perhaps it is a special room, that is always here so people who love the Ring Fire can always find a safe place to be. But it could also be somewhere that the Fire Giver has created to keep Kern's mother, Claire, safe. We've no way of knowing but, if we can find it, we may discover some clue as to where or what the Ring's End may be. That should lead us to the Fire Giver himself, then we can ask him what to do about the trial of magic in the morning.'

'I wish we could just refuse to take part,' Gemma said sadly. 'But that would be the same as conceding. I do feel that Rowanne was right about one thing, though.'

'What was that?' Phelan asked.

'That, somehow, the Ring Fire will win in the end. If we make a mess of things tomorrow, it may take a little longer and someone else to make things turn out as they ought, but everything *will* be all right in the end.'

'The trouble is,' Fleabag added ruefully, 'that one story's end is the beginning of another. Once one situation is sorted out, it inevitably becomes the gateway to the next lot of problems. There won't ever be a "happily ever after" until we reach the Fire Giver's own world, the Land Beyond.'

'Oh my, you do sound doleful this evening.' Gemma gave her friend a playful rub behind his ears that made him purr warmly. 'Now, how do we start looking? Kern, you know this place well. Have you any ideas?'

'No. This turret room was my only bet, and that was wrong. But what I *do* know is that although this building looks square and ordinary from the outside, it's constructed very cunningly. Instead of being a simple four-sided design, like the others in the University, it's actually a star shape on the inside, and in some places it can fold and tuck in on itself, so when you think you are walking in one direction, you're actually going somewhere completely different. It causes chaos amongst new servants; some have been known to go missing for weeks at a time! Domnall showed me how to get around when I was quite little.

'There is a knack to it: you must not be afraid of how odd things may *seem* and you have to think clearly at all costs. It has nothing to do with magic, and a lot to do with courage. It was built that way to confuse intruders, and as a test of determination for people who came here wanting to study. That was in the days when a wizard was simply a wise man or woman, not a practitioner of evil arts.'

'So we must all stay close to you, Kern,' Phelan said. 'Do we have to go all the way down to the ground floor again?'

Kern laughed. 'No, it's easier than that.' And he opened a door in the wall that no one had noticed before. Beyond was a long attic room filled with servants sleeping in their truckle beds. Bewildered, Gemma, Phelan and Fleabag looked back into the turret room behind them. There it was, with windows on every wall, looking out high over the roofs.

They were way above anywhere that could possibly join to another part of the building.

Kern put his finger to his lips and whispered, 'As I said, don't be afraid, and stay together. We won't lose each other as long as we stay in the same room as each other. Hold onto someone else as you step through the door. If one of us steps over a threshold without the others, it could take for ever to catch up again.' And with that he quietly walked from the turret room into the attic ahead.

He nodded. 'We can let go now. Then he set about very softly opening the two doors at the far end of the attic. 'No, no sign of the room here. Follow me.'

Kern bent down and pushed a rug aside. There in the floor was a trapdoor. He pulled on the iron ring and softly lowered the cover back until it rested on the floor. 'Come quickly, and hold on!'

Phelan put his hand on the boy's shoulder and Gemma grabbed Phelan's shirt. Fleabag jumped onto Gemma's shoulder as she bent down to slide through the opening.

The next room was a long, stone-arched gallery, lit by blue flaming torches in wall brackets. Kern led the way down the wooden stair from the trapdoor. As Gemma let the wooden cover fall back into place, it closed with a click. She looked back up at it, but there was no sign that there had even been a way through the ceiling.

'Ugh!' she exclaimed as she jumped down from the ladder. 'This is beginning to give me the creeps!' And then the ladder disappeared.

The gallery had doorways between each stone arch on the left, and on the right, a long row of lancet windows, tall, plain and with thick rounded pillars between each one. The friends spread out along the length of the gallery, opening doorways and peering through the windows. The first few looked out over a moonlight garden, but then the scenes began to change.

Sometimes the explorers found themselves watching a feast in what appeared to be a private dining room, yet the next window which was scarcely a man's handspan away, showed a practice yard with knights fencing or wrestling in broad day-light in summer.

'How much of this is real?' Gemma asked.

Kern just shrugged. 'As real as anything the wizards do,' he replied. 'If we go to the end of here, we should get to the centre of the star, and from there it might be easier to find our way onwards. But whatever you do, stay in contact with each other as you go through doorways, and if a path looks impossible keep going. Remember, things are not as they seem!'

Gemma threw a worried glance at Phelan. For the first time, she was wondering whether Kern was to be trusted, and if his story about his mother and him being the unwanted relations of the old Chancellor had been a complicated lie to lead them all into a trap.

Gemma opened her hand and looked at the Ring Fire while she thought of Kern. It was burning small and clear. She closed her hand again. Kern was not a traitor, but was this the way to find the small room with the stone fireplace? She was about to look into the Ring Fire again, when suddenly guards rushed in, yelling challenges.

Kern put his fiddle to his shoulder and drew the bow across the strings. Gemma did not wait to put the plugs in her ears; she grabbed Fleabag, put her hand on Phelan's shoulder and ran through the nearest doorway with Kern hot on her heels...

The Great Hall was the last place Gemma wanted to be. It was the room where Rowanne's initiation had taken place, as well as Fleabag's trial of wisdom and wit. It was also the room that was built to imitate the Hall of Light back at Harflorum, the very room where she, Phelan and Fleabag had defeated the old Chancellor. It had been rebuilt since the fire, of course, but every time they came there since, visions of the coloured magics he had thrown at them always flashed through her memory.

Thankfully the hall was empty.

Kern walked straight to the central point, which was more or less where Fleabag's red-gold cushion had been placed the day before. Then he put his violin to his shoulder and began to play a different sort of music, one that cleared the mind. 'Think!' he said urgently. 'Think of the room, and we will find our way to it.'

But as the image of the room and its strange fire-place began to drift through their minds M'Kinnik ran into the hall, with his arms raised, already chanting a spell.

Kern turned and played his music for all he was worth, subtly changing the tune from one that cleared the head to a different melody, that was so complex and intertwining that no one could think at all.

Gemma had been clenching her fists, trying to concentrate on the image of the Ring Fire burning around the friends, protecting them from M'Kinnik's malice, when she saw him hesitate and falter, stumbling and stroking his chin as he tried to remember what it was he had been trying to say or do.

'Quick!' hissed Kern, 'this way', and he slipped through a tiny wooden door set into a thick, carved pillar.

Kern did not miss a note as he pushed the door wider with his knee, and Gemma, Phelan and Fleabag slid behind him into a long, vaulted hall.

'Phew!' sighed Kern as he leaned against the wall, eyes closed, and the fiddle hanging loosely at his side. 'That was close!'

Gemma, Fleabag and Phelan did not reply, for M'Kinnik and his wizards were straight ahead – less than a wand's length away.

21

Descending into Darkness

Kern played frantically as he ran straight through the crowd of blue-clad men and women. Heads nodded and knees sank as his music swept across them like a soporific wind.

Phelan and Gemma kept as close as they could behind Kern, but Fleabag could not keep up on his three legs. Gemma turned and grabbed him, just as Kern was stepping through a doorway that had suddenly appeared only a few steps ahead of them. She took hold of Phelan's coat again just as he crossed the threshold.

They found themselves standing inside the top of a dizzy-looking tower with a narrow stone stair twisting away below. Gemma gulped. She did not like heights, and on their left was just a black space. There was no handrail, just cold, dark nothingness.

'Kern... Kern, I think there's something you ought to know...' Her voice sounded shaky as she tried to take a few steps downwards.

'Yes?' The sound of their feet echoed up from out of the gloom. Gemma groped her hand down the cold stone wall on the right and tried not to think of the slippery steps under her feet.

'What is it?' Kern's voice drifted up out of the depths. It sounded so far away, muffled by the echoing tread of their feet.

'It's just that...' Gemma tried hard not to look down. She gulped. Her head was swimming, she was certain she was going to fall... or even worse, to fling herself down into the void. She was feeling sick, so she stopped and turned to face the cold wall. She clutched Fleabag so tightly he mewed. She couldn't walk and talk at the same time.

'Stop, please!' She called urgently. 'I've got to tell you that every time we think we have put our pursuers to sleep, we haven't. When I turned to pick Fleabag up just then, M'Kinnik and all his followers were fading away. They are just *sendings*. They aren't real. Somewhere in this place, the real wizards are watching us, and we are running round and round, exhausting ourselves, like mice on a wheel. They are playing with us, Kern!'

The boy stopped. Gemma could hear him breathing hard. Although they were standing in almost pitch black, the violin glowed an eerie blue.

Fleabag pushed his furry face into Gemma's ear. 'Light the Ring Fire, Gemma. I'm certain Kern doesn't mean to, but I think he's leading us the wrong way.'

Gemma passed Fleabag onto Phelan's shoulder. 'You take him, I need both hands free,' she said. Then, standing with her back to the wall, she held out her right hand so the Ring Fire gave a strong, golden light. But what they saw made them gasp, for instead of standing on a stair spiralling down into terrifying empty space, they now found a floor on their left, with a stone wall and a wide, oak door slightly ajar.

Without thinking, Gemma stepped down from the stair and pushed the door wider. It creaked on its hinges. It was solid. The floor was solid.

'Hey,' she whispered. 'This way. The Ring Fire wants us to go in here.'

'Careful,' Kern warned. 'I've never found a doorway at that point before. It could be a trick, maybe even another sending. You'll be killed if you take a wrong turn here; that empty space below us is real – I promise.'

But Gemma was already halfway through the doorway, with Phelan and Fleabag close behind her. Kern did not hesitate, but ran back up the last steps and jumped in through the entrance, just as it disappeared.

Inside, the glow from the Ring Fire in Gemma's hands was bathing everything with a warm golden light.

For one second, Gemma was hopeful that they had found their strange little room for by the light of the Ring Fire they could see it was very similarly built. This room was quite bare, and circular, constructed from close-fitting blocks of plain, white stone. All around were tall, lancet windows, shuttered against the bleak, black night outside. The wind howled, rattling at the shutter catches. Gemma instinctively stepped towards the grate, to see if there were coals that could be stirred to some sort of life. But the fire had long died. A few ashes and

160

lumps of black charcoal were all that was left. Gemma stared at the stone mantelpiece, and shook her head. Something was very familiar about it, but also very wrong, all at the same time.

This was not the place they were looking for.

Just then, the wind blew even harder, lashing the outer walls and wailing. The door creaked open, then slammed shut. The Ring Fire flickered in Gemma's hands and, for a split second, everything was dark. Then the golden light sprang back, revealing a tall, dark-swathed figure, standing in the very centre of the room.

Kern raised his left hand and lifted his violin towards his shoulder.

But the figure stepped forward and put a dark gloved hand across the strings. 'Don't touch it, whatever you do,' a familiar voice warned.

'Rowanne!' Gemma gasped. 'Are you all right? What are you doing here?'

The Princess, draped in blue-black from head to toe, pulled her hood forward and shielded her eyes from the sight of the Ring Fire. 'I hoped I would catch up with you. Kern uses these secret ways very skilfully. But he kept playing the violin so I couldn't get close.'

'Was that because it reminded you of the Ring Fire? Does it hurt when Kern plays it?' Phelan asked kindly.

'No, on the contrary,' Rowanne replied. 'It is infused with Blue Magic. It summoned me, but it also summoned every other wizard for miles around. I didn't want them to find me trying to help you.'

'Thank you for all the help you've tried to give us

so far, especially for the sword…' Phelan began.

But the dark figure put a finger to her lips. 'Hush, there is no time to talk now. Kern or whatever your name is, give me the fiddle. Every time you play it, you might as well wave a flag, blow a trumpet and shout, "Kern is here!"'

'Oh I don't know; it's not so bad now it has decent strings on it,' Fleabag said. 'I'd have agreed with you when it had Great-Aunt Bertha's guts strung on it. I never liked Bertha particularly, but I didn't think it was right for Kern to play jigs on her intestines.'

Phelan glowered at the cat, then glanced at Kern. The boy looked deeply hurt as he clutched his most treasured – and probably only – possession in the whole world to his chest, and scowled.

Rowanne spread her hands and looked appealingly at Phelan. 'Surely you know that Domnall gave it to him. Even if the person who plays it is playing the Ring Fire's own music, the instrument itself is made with magic. Did I not warn you that everything that was wizard-blue would ultimately betray you? Why do you think I wouldn't let Kern bring that thing from Harflorum when we left? Even though I had no training at that stage, I could sense that it was dangerous, and that the wizards wanted Kern to have it. I did not know why at the time, but I do now.

'They can't use it to *do* magic, only to be aware of where you are and what you're playing. They've been following you all evening. And what's more, you've been giving away who you really are with every note you play. You've got to give it to me, or at least stop playing it!'

Rowanne stretched out her hand, but Kern cowered back, clutching his fiddle so tightly he almost snapped it again.

'No!' he shouted, 'No! It's not true! You're lying!'

Phelan, Fleabag and Gemma stared at Kern. When Kern saw they believed Rowanne, he tried to slide towards the door.

'How *dare* you say such things?' he howled. 'Domnall was my brother. He was the only person who ever cared about me.'

Rowanne shook her head. 'Domnall didn't give it to you to be kind. He gave it to you to trap you. Isn't that so?'

Kern turned red and stamped. 'No! He gave it to me because he knew I loved music. I'll never part with it, never!' And with that he turned and ran through the door by which they had entered.

Phelan, Gemma and Fleabag weren't quick enough to catch hold of him as he went through. Without him they had no idea of how to get back. There was no point trying to retrace their steps.

'Bother!' Fleabag moaned. 'Now we'll have to get back a different way, and I'd just spotted a nice juicy rat before the door slammed.'

'How could you think of your stomach at a time like this?' Gemma chided.

'Quite easily,' the cat replied. 'It never stops thinking about me, so why should I forget *it*?'

Rowanne laughed, but it was not a merry sound. It was as lost and lonely as the wind outside the walls. 'Dear Fleabag,' she said with genuine affection, 'I expect when you get back to your study, you will find supper laid out just as you ordered it.'

'But where *is* our study?' Fleabag scratched himself behind an ear. 'Even with my super feline sense of direction, all this folded space and the twisted dimensions we've been through have thrown me entirely. Where are we, and how do we get back?'

'This way,' Rowanne moved a stone in the wall to one side with a light touch and, as she did so, another stone moved on the other side, making an opening wide enough even for Phelan's broad shoulders.

Fleabag jumped through first, followed by Gemma and Phelan. Ahead was the warm glow of the study fire, and an evening meal laid out, just as Rowanne had promised.

'Thank you, Rowanne,' Gemma said, 'I know you really are trying to help, it just seems to have all gone terribly wrong.'

The Chancellor nodded. 'I know,' she replied, but her voice sounded choked.

Just then Phelan had a thought and put his head back through the opening. 'Rowanne, what did you mean by the violin being a trap for Kern?'

Rowanne was just a dark smudge in a darker darkness now the Ring Fire had left the room with Gemma. She raised her arms. 'Ask Kern. She knows the truth.'

At that moment, the door behind them opened, and Kern slipped in, looking pale and frightened. Phelan turned back to speak to Rowanne again, but she was not there. They were staring at a bookcase with a small gap where a few volumes had fallen down.

22

The Woman of Flowers

Kern sank miserably into a deep leather armchair –
and got up again very quickly, apologizing profusely.
Fleabag disliked being used as a cushion by any
human – even Phelan.

The boy paced the room swinging his fiddle
between his fingers as he walked. Once or twice he
raised it to his shoulder, but lowered it again, as he
caught Phelan's warning look.

The boy glowered back at the King. 'But I *need* to
play it or I'll explode. You don't understand!' he
sulked. 'I just can't stand *not* playing it.'

Gemma put a small flicker of Ring Fire onto the
candle on the table. 'Watch the glow, it will help to
calm you,' she said kindly. 'We're not unsympathetic
– it's just too dangerous. For you as well as for us.'

Kern pushed his violin behind a chair and turned
his back on them all, staring out of the window into
the wintry blackness beyond. Snow flung itself at the
window panes like millions of white bees endlessly
swarming around and around, until Kern began to
feel dizzy. He rested his head on the glass and fought
the sting of tears in his eyes.

Just as he had decided to go to bed and try to forget everything until the morning, Gemma suddenly gave a shout. 'How *could* we have been so stupid?'

'Speak for yourself,' Fleabag groaned as he rolled over on the chair to stretch and grin up at his friend.

'Well, you've been daft too!' she teased. 'Look!' then she jumped up and pranced around the room, swinging her arms this way and that. 'Well?' she shouted triumphantly, 'what do you notice?'

'That you've gone nuttier than a fruit cake and battier than a belfry!' Fleabag replied. 'Either that, or you've decided to launch a new career as a pigeon, and can't wait to start.'

'No *look!*' she demanded, beginning her tour of the room one more time. '*Look*! *This* is a circular room! It is just that there are so many book cases and bits of cluttery furniture in here, we never noticed before! It even has lancet windows too, as well as a huge old stone fireplace...' She ran across the room and traced the worn edges of an ancient carved pattern springing up from the floor, and intertwining across the front of the fireplace, under the mantelpiece. 'Look!' Gemma explained, 'this is a very faint version of the tree design we saw in the circular room where Claire lay.

'Now I know what was wrong with the room where we met Rowanne just now; everything was inside out. The carving was there too, but it was all done backwards – parts that should have stuck out were indented. It was all negative – the opposite of what it should have been.'

'I see...' Phelan said, running his fingers over the

carved stonework. 'And the windows were dark and shuttered, instead of light and open. It felt cold and lonely, instead of contented and peaceful!'

'But this isn't *quite* the room, either,' Gemma went on.

'But *that* is,' said Fleabag, peering through the flames of the fire.

Gemma and Phelan both knelt down on the faded old hearthrug to look through the grate from a cat's-eye point of view.

'Well I never!' whistled Phelan. 'It was here all the time!'

'The answers usually are,' Gemma added quietly. 'That's why it's so difficult to find them – because they are under our noses.'

'Well, *I* knew all along, of course,' Fleabag added in a superior voice.

'Then why didn't you tell us?' Phelan demanded, picking the cat up by the scruff of the neck and glaring into his big golden eyes.

'Just testing,' he replied, cheekily. 'But I told you in the end because it became tedious watching you all running around this place like kittens chasing their tails.'

Phelan threw back his head and laughed heartily. 'Well, at least thanks to your leadership, redoubtable mog, we might be somewhere near finding the Fire Giver now. I will definitely have to knight you all over again and get you that second golden earring!

'Now, if only we could get through to that other room, we might find a clue as to where the Ring's End is,' and Phelan leaned low under the mantelpiece and peered through the flames once again.

'Can you see my mother there?' Kern asked quietly.

'Hold on a moment,' Phelan replied, leaning further in. 'I'm trying to see.'

Gemma tugged at her friend's shirt and pulled him back. 'Careful, you'll catch fire. Your beard and hair were right in the flames just now...' Then she looked at the King's face and clothes. 'But you're not even singed,' she said quietly. Then she stretched out her own hand into the flames. Instead of snatching it back quickly, she held it in the heart of the fire, quite calmly.

'Phelan,' she said, after a few moments. 'How could I have been so stupid? I lit this fire myself. It is no ordinary flame, it is Ring Fire, and it's letting us through. We are free to go to the other side if we wish – and if we have the courage.'

Within seconds, Phelan had crawled under the mantelpiece with the golden flames licking his breeches and shoes. But the fire did not even scorch the cloth. Fleabag followed quickly, with Kern and Gemma close behind.

As Gemma straightened, she rubbed her eyes, for the sunlight streaming in through the tall lancet windows all around the little room was very bright. She dusted the grimy streaks from her dress and pushed her hair back out of her eyes.

The first thing she noticed was that there were more people in the room than had come through the fireplace. Under one window was an elegant chaise-longue, and on it, dressed in a green brocade gown, was a beautiful young woman, fast asleep. Kern noticed her too, and went over and touched the sleeper's cheek. 'Mother?' he asked. 'Where have all your rags gone? You look like a lady now! Mother, wake up! It's me, I've come to get you.'

'Not yet,' came a creaky voice from near the fire. Kern and Gemma turned to see an old, old, dark-skinned woman with fine, white, wispy hair, dressed in a gown covered in blossoms, so exquisitely sewn that they looked quite real.

She was seated by the fire in front of a tambour frame, sewing a half-finished tapestry of a field of tangled wild flowers.

'Your mother is still sleeping,' the strange flower-woman said, nodding towards Kern. 'She'll come to you when the time is right, and when the truth is told.' Then she smiled, folding the ancient skin on her face into a million wrinkles. 'And who knows? Perhaps it is almost time for both things to happen, eh?' and she cackled a merry laugh that seemed to make the sun shine even more brightly into the little room.

Then she turned her dark, wrinkled face towards Phelan and Gemma, her sloe-black eyes twinkling. She pointed a long, bony finger in their direction. 'And what do you two want, eh?'

Phelan found himself lost for words, but Gemma knelt down on the hearthrug and looked up at the old woman. 'I can't think where, but I've seen you before…'

'Of course you have and of course you haven't, my dear. Now, it's getting late. Tell me why you're here. This thread is getting very short.' And then she began to sew so fast that no one could even see her hand, it was a complete blur. But the fine scarlet thread between her fingers stayed clear and bright, although visibly shrinking every second.

'I can't keep the gateway open any longer than this thread,' the old woman said, 'so tell me quickly what it is you want.'

Gemma stared at the fine silk, and then at the brightness in the black eyes. Now she knew where she had seen it before: in so many places and times, but most of all four years ago, in the Hall of Light at Harflorum. She had to find the courage to be honest and ask for what she needed, just as she had that night when she had first spoken to the Ring Fire.

'We need to find a champion for the trial of magic tomorrow, and we need to find the Ring's End,' she blurted out, all in one breath.

The old woman peered at Gemma over her tapestry, then suddenly she stopped sewing. Quite kindly, but very firmly, she said, 'Go back. You have everything you need, although all is not what it seems. As I said before, all will be revealed when the truth is told, and your poor friend Rowanne has already told it to you once. But, as to the other, your King friend has *that* under his nose. It has often been under yours as well, my dear, but at the moment, it is all around you.

'Now goodnight. Go and get some sleep. You will need it.' And the old woman bent over and kissed Gemma on the head. Gemma twisted herself around to go through the fire again, for she could see the scarlet thread was getting impossibly short, although somehow the old woman kept on sewing with it. But as she glanced at the mantelpiece, she gasped, for the carving on it was the same as on the other side of the fire, but sharp and freshly cut as if the mason had only finished his work that day. It was an intricately cut woodland, with intertwining branches and every individual leaf shaped with such precision and love it seemed almost alive.

She hesitated. She didn't want to leave. Phelan knelt on the rug beside her and gently pushed Gemma onwards.

'Time to go, time to go!' the old woman chided. 'It is midnight,' and she picked up her scissors to cut the thread.

But as the friends passed through the flames, they heard Fleabag asking, 'Mistress, when I see you again, may I sleep on your lap?'

'Of course,' the reply came. 'For ever, if you like.'

Gemma reached the hearthrug in the study and glanced backwards, but all she saw was the back of the fireplace. There *was* no other room. Scared in case the fire should burn her, she kicked hard, and stubbed her toe on the stonework. Phelan grabbed her by her arm and pulled her up.

Fleabag was already curled up on the hearthrug, snoring gently, and Kern was nowhere to be seen.

'Well, what was that all about?' Gemma sat down and stared into the fire in amazement.

'I think,' Phelan said slowly. 'I think, though I'm not sure, that we just met the Fire Giver herself.'

'Himself,' Gemma corrected absently. Then she sat up straight, wide-eyed. 'But if that's true, and *she* was the Fire Giver, then where is the Ring's End?'

23

Rowanne's Visit

In the morning, a maid knocked on the door with breakfast.

Phelan opened the door, bleary-eyed, and Fleabag shot past into the corridor. The guard challenged him, but he yelled out, 'I need the garden quick!' and slipped through their legs.

Gemma woke and stared out of the window at the leaden skies above. A few minutes later, Fleabag bounced in with cold wet paws and snow-covered fur. He jumped on Gemma's bed and rubbed his grubbiness all over her face and hands.

'Go away, you horrid animal!' she groaned, trying to roll over.

Fleabag ignored her protests. 'Time to get up. We only have four hours to go.'

Gemma did not feel like getting up. She reached out and scratched Fleabag absently behind one ear and smiled rather ruefully. 'I'm scared, old friend. What happens if we don't make it?'

'Then we don't. There's a whole world of cats and humans out there, who all have their part to play. We will do our best for them. If we win we win, and if we don't, it'll be their turn next. No reason to be all morose and not get up.' The cat started to knead his claws in and out of Gemma's chest.

'Ouch!' she squealed, pushing him away. 'Get off me, you assassin. I'll call the guard!'

But Fleabag jumped back and settled under Gemma's chin, where he began to lick her with his hot rough tongue. 'Come on, if you shift now, I'll share my mackerel with you, and that's a promise. Though it is a bit old. I suspect we don't get the best service in this place. I'm glad my poor, dear wife Tabitha isn't here. All this second-rate food would upset her digestion terribly.'

'I bet you do wish Tabitha was here,' Gemma smiled. She could not remember anything about her own family, and she rather envied Fleabag's endless tumbles of kittens that were always getting under everyone's feet at the palace in Harflorum. She had Fleabag's talking sons Hereward and Rufus to keep her company in her cottage in the rocks, but sometimes she did feel very alone. Especially this morning. So much rested on *her*.

Fleabag jumped down and ran towards the study. But, just as he was about to disappear around the door, he turned back. 'Actually, I'm *very* glad Tabitha isn't here,' he admitted. 'Even I am finding all this a little scary.'

Gemma made herself get out from under the warm covers and pull on a dressing gown. She could hear voices in the next room and wondered who their visitor could be. The University servants never spoke when they brought coal or food.

She pushed the door wider and looked in. A tall,

dark-cloaked figure stood hunched by the door, with a deep hood pulled down low over its face. Could it really be Rowanne? How could she bear to come into the study? Perhaps she wore the hood to hide the sight of the Ring Fire from her eyes.

'Good morning, Rowanne, how are you?' Gemma smiled, and held a hand out in greeting.

Rowanne ignored the hand, and seemed, if possible, to shrink even more into her hood. 'Fleabag came and fetched me this morning. He said you wanted to see me,' she said simply.

'It was all his idea,' Phelan replied, getting up from the breakfast table. 'But it was a good one. We just wanted to say that, whatever happens, Rowanne, we thank you for all your help and your faithful friendship over the years. And if you want to come back with us, we would love to have you with us again...'

Gemma hung her head. Rowanne was so drenched in the blue magic, there was barely a shred of her real self left. Could their old friend ever be happy with them again? 'Yes, of course,' she managed to say, because she really did wish it were possible.

There was a long uncomfortable silence. 'My offer is still open,' Rowanne said at last.

'What offer is that?' Gemma asked.

'To help you with the trial of magic. I can't fight it for you, as you know, but I can help you... That's why I went through all this in the first place... to help the Ring Fire.'

Suddenly Gemma saw red. She was *not* going to let Rowanne get away with this self-righteousness any longer. That could not have been the reason – at least, not the whole reason – for her becoming a wizard. She stood squarely in front of her old friend, hands on hips, and head held high. 'What else was behind all this, Rowanne? If helping the Ring Fire was your only motive, however misguided, you just could not have become as – well – as *blue* as you are! Loving the Ring Fire and becoming a cauldron-stirring, spell-throwing wizard, don't mix. It just can't happen! The Blue Magic only works for evil and for controlling people, but the Ring Fire always helps good things to happen.'

Rowanne hung her head and muttered, 'Witches stir cauldrons, not wizards!'

'Oh, so *what*!' Gemma stamped her foot. 'You know perfectly well what I mean. Why did you do it? Knowing the real Rowanne, I can quite believe that wanting to help the Ring Fire by doing something very practical was at least part of your becoming a wizard – but what else is going on inside you, Rowanne? If you can face whatever it is, you might be able to find a way out of this. For sure as eggs are eggs, I can't see us taking you back with us the way you are. As you yourself have told us several times, whatever is wizard-blue will ultimately betray us.'

At the end of this speech, Gemma was pink in the face and quite breathless, but she stood her ground, waiting for a reply, undaunted by the sinister shape of her old friend.

But Rowanne said nothing. She did not stir or even lift her head. She just stayed quite still and began to crackle and fizz with minute blue sparks like a tiny electrical storm. Then she began to fade, slowly at first, but after a few seconds the process speeded up, as if an unseen hand was angrily rubbing her out. Quite suddenly what was left of her disappeared with a small 'pop' of blue sparks – and she was gone.

Phelan came and quietly took Gemma's elbow and drew her away to sit on the settee.

Fleabag jumped up and looked Phelan in the eye. 'I know Rowanne and I have had our differences, but I do love her. She's been a first rate cat-hater all her life. I wish there was something I could do.' And a tear rolled down his untidy furry face.

Phelan shook his head and stroked Fleabag, pushing away moisture at the corners of his own eyes. 'You were a bit harsh, don't you think?' He frowned. 'Even the Fire Giver called Rowanne our "poor friend". If *she* can have sympathy for her, *we* should give Rowanne another chance too. Somehow we've got to trust the old Rowanne is still deep inside the blue wizard. She's been incredibly brave coming to see us at all. I'm certain she only wants to help, even if her motives are muddled. There must be a corner of her that isn't completely absorbed by the wizards' magic.'

Gemma felt her cheeks go hot. 'You're right. I'm sorry. Perhaps her longing to help the Ring Fire will still win out in the end.'

'But we haven't got time to worry about it this morning,' Fleabag reminded them. 'Breakfast is getting cold and we have the most important trial of all at noon.'

Gemma sat at the table. She felt miserable and lonely. She toyed with her food and stared into the fire. What had happened last night? Had they dreamed going through the fire into the small room with the strange old woman?

Phelan followed her gaze and answered her thoughts. 'We did go through, we did see Claire, and we did see the Fire Giver.'

'Are you certain?'

'Certain we went through or that it was the Fire Giver?'

'Certain of any of it?' Gemma had never really had any image of what the Fire Giver might or might not be like – except perhaps fiery in some way. 'Certain that we "have everything we need, but that all is not what it seems"? And what is that truth that must be told that Rowanne has already told us?'

Gemma looked across at Fleabag who had his nose in a dish of cream on the hearthrug. The cat looked back at Gemma, eyes wide. He shrugged. 'Don't look at me. I'm no good at riddles. I thought you knew that!' and he returned his face to the bowl where he made awful slurping noises with his tongue.

Suddenly, Gemma looked up. 'Has anyone seen Kern this morning? What did that old woman mean by "the truth being told" when she was talking to him? None of it makes any sense!' And she began to stir her tea so hard that the cup began to rock.

Phelan got up and put his arms around her shoulders. 'It will be all right, I promise. What matters is that we have been promised that we will have all we need to meet the trial. I don't know where the Ring's End is, but I'm certain we were there last night and we met the Fire Giver. But perhaps he – or she – isn't quite what any of us imagines or expects; she may not

177

look like an old woman next time we see her.'

Gemma rubbed her nose on the sleeve of her dressing gown. 'That's all very well as fine words and stuff. And I'm sure you're right: when you lived with wise old Aelforth you learned more about the Ring Fire than I shall ever know. But what do I do now... today... this morning?

'I can't help feeling that I am expected to take the trial of magic because I'm the Fire Wielder. But I know in my bones that I mustn't do it... So what do I do? Just sit up here and watch the clock tick by, one minute to twelve, twelve o'clock, one minute past...? Tell me, Phelan, Fleabag... What do I *do*?' And she burst into tears and ran into her bedroom, slamming the door behind her.

Phelan and Fleabag looked at each other. 'I know how she feels,' admitted the King.

'So do I,' replied the cat. 'Will you open the door so I can go and curl up next to her? Humans sometimes like a cuddle when they're feeling bad.'

Phelan let Fleabag into Gemma's room, then he sat in the study all alone, and drank tea.

24

Battle Lines

Gemma stood up and tried to breathe calmly. The knock on the door told her it was time for her armed escort to take her down to the Great Hall to face this last and most frightening trial.

All morning, Phelan had tried to get messages to his men in the barracks to have the horses ready for a sudden flight. But no communication was allowed. They tried to find the secret bookcase passageway out of their study that they had used the night before. But without Kern or Rowanne, they were stuck. They could not discern any opening, or any way of making one appear. They were truly imprisoned.

Their windows were too high for even the redoubtable Fleabag to jump down and so he had pleaded to be allowed to use the garden. But he was pushed back into the room and given a dirt box, which did them no good at all. 'I'm not using that anyway,' he sniffed contemptuously. 'Dirt boxes are for kittens and invalids. I'll go on M'Kinnik's lap if I get caught short!'

Gemma had tried to calm her thoughts. She had

to at least turn up for this trial, even though she still felt very strongly that she should take no part in it. 'Perhaps the Fire Giver will provide her own Champion,' Phelan suggested. 'She did say we had everything we needed. So perhaps something we haven't thought of yet will happen, right under our noses.'

'Like the Ring's End is under *your* nose!' Gemma managed a smile.

'Exactly!' Phelan laughed. 'It's almost time to go. Are you ready? The worst that can happen is that we will have a draw. Then the fight will go on another day, in another way.'

'No,' Gemma said quietly. 'That's not the worst that can happen.' And she walked out of the door, with a blue-clad guard on either side.

Gemma had decided to dress as she had done for the time she had played the Fire Maiden with Fleabag as her 'terrifying' black cat. She wore a flame-red silk dress, and a plain woollen cloak. 'Perhaps,' she had explained to Fleabag, 'the memories of how we defeated the old Chancellor will still be fresh in some people's minds. It wasn't that long ago. It might give us a slight advantage.'

'We'll see,' grunted Fleabag, slipping between the guards' legs to lead the procession with his strange, lopsided three-legged walk. He held his tail high like a scruffy black banner, and spread his whiskers wide. The wizards did not like cats, particularly black ones. Perhaps Gemma's idea might do some good, especially if he was there as well...

Phelan came behind, walking tall and dressed like a king in his full regalia. He had not been allowed to come armed, and had reluctantly left Rowanne's sword behind. He was worried that the wizards might somehow force or trick Fleabag's true name from him, allowing them to put a spell on his best friend. Gemma was safe; she had no knowledge of her real name, and although he could remember the name his parents had given him at birth – well, he didn't matter. If the wizards put a spell on him, as long as Gemma and Fleabag were safe, that was all that was important.

The King lifted his head and followed the procession along the winding corridors to the Great Hall, built to imitate the wonderful Hall of Light at home in Harflorum. Whatever was about to happen would be over very soon now. But he couldn't help wondering whether Kern was all right, and where he was. He would have liked to help him find his mother and to escape. He would have offered him a home at Harflorum. But he put the boy out of his mind. He had to concentrate. He had to give Gemma all his attention. He glanced down at the Great Ring of office, the huge opal that all the kings and queens of the land wore.

It glowed richly with the deep golden-red of the Ring Fire, and comforted him. If only the answer to the Fire Giver's riddle was as plainly under his nose as the Ring. He might be able to help Gemma, if only he could work out what was meant by the old lady's riddles. For Phelan was in no doubt that even if she *wasn't* the Fire Giver then she was at least one of his (or her) friends.

They reached the Great Hall. Gemma was led to a seat in the exact centre, with wizards, in rustling blue gowns of every shade, thronging in all around.

'It's a good job we're not relying on magic,' Fleabag muttered. 'You'd need a powerful lot of it to defeat this crowd!'

A trumpet blast announced the arrival of her Holiness, the High Chancellor of All Wizards, her Ladyship, Princess Rowanne de Montiland. Rowanne swept in between the crowds to sit in a lapis-studded throne opposite Gemma. Guards tried to force Gemma to bow to Rowanne, but she would not, despite their kicks and prods.

'Leave her!' the Chancellor ordered. 'It will soon be over. Obeisance does not matter.'

Gemma looked hard at Rowanne. Was this a sending or the real thing? Was it Rowanne at all or just some blue creature who looked like her? The features looked the same, and the blue-black hair was tightly drawn back as if their old friend was about to pull on a woollen snood and put her helmet on. How much stronger and more beautiful she looked when she was being herself in battle gear as a Lady Knight, than in all these silks and satins with blue embroidery and encrusting gems. Gemma was very sad, but what Rowanne felt she could not guess.

The Chancellor rose to her feet and signalled to Gemma to do the same. Then she spoke, clearly and loudly. 'Be it known that the outcome of this trial will decide the fate of the sovereignty of the land and the ownership of the Ring Fire for ever.

'If I win, then all is ours, for ever. If the Lady Gemma Streetchild or her Champion wins, then everything belongs to the Fire Wielders and their chosen monarchs for ever, and the Noble Order of

Wizards will unravel their magic so it can never be rewoven again.'

'So be it,' responded the wizards, roaring so loudly that the foundations of the hall shook.

'So be it,' Gemma, Phelan and Fleabag said as clearly as they could, although they could hardly speak. Then Gemma swallowed hard and added: 'But, my Lady Chancellor, you must know that even if we lose, we cannot *give* you the Fire. It owns itself. It goes where it will. It can never be owned or used like magic.' Gemma comforted herself with the thought that whatever deals the wizards tried to make were irrelevant. The wizards would never even be able to look at it, let alone 'have' it.

Rowanne's face did not change its set expression, but M'Kinnik scowled as he settled himself next to her.

Fleabag jumped up onto Gemma's arm-rest and pawed at her elbow. 'Have courage. Whatever happens today, all will be well.'

'Thanks, Sir Scrag-Belly,' Gemma tried to smile as she sat. Then she thought of something, and stood again to speak. 'Just one more thing, my Lady – what if there is a draw, as on the other two days?' she asked.

Rowanne leaned forward, and lifted her right hand so all the spectators could see the huge, dead opal on her own finger, the one that Chancellors always wore, longing to contain the Ring Fire at its depths. 'There will be no draw,' she said simply. 'Not this time.' Then the Chancellor sat back and folded her hands, 'I understand, my Lady Fire Wielder, that you do not wish to take this trial yourself. Where is your Champion?'

Gemma took a deep breath. This was it. The time to admit they had no Champion, and she knew now more clearly than anything she had ever known in her life that she must not fight Rowanne. As soon as she spoke the words, the trial would be lost. By the laws of Challenge combat, they would have conceded total defeat.

Gemma's heart was pounding fast as she opened her mouth. She fixed her gaze on Rowanne and took a deep breath.

Suddenly, from the back of the hall, a small voice called out: 'I am their Champion. I will take this trial for the Ring Fire!'

25

The Champion

Every head in the room turned this way and that to see who had spoken. Gemma and Phelan exchanged astounded looks. Fleabag simply slipped into Gemma's empty chair, which had a very comfortable, although rather blue-coloured cushion. 'Good,' he purred. 'I thought she'd do it. Time for forty winks while the fuss dies down.' And he went to sleep.

Guards soon cleared a path in the thronging hall for a girl in a long white dress, with a green veil over her head and a green silk bundle under her arm. She came and stood before Gemma and bowed. 'My Lady Fire Wielder, I ask your permission to fight the Blue Magic on your behalf.'

Gemma did not know what to say. She opened her right hand very quickly, and saw a small flame of Ring Fire burning with a brilliance and intensity that she had never seen before, except maybe the day she was proclaimed Fire Wielder in the Hall of Light. Whoever this girl was didn't matter. The Ring Fire accepted her. As Fleabag had promised, all was very well indeed. 'I agree,' she answered clearly.

Then the stranger turned to Rowanne and bowed again. 'My Lady Chancellor, I ask your leave to be your opponent in this trial.'

Rowanne nodded. 'I accept.'

Gemma glanced around. Who was this girl? Why was she veiled? What did the colour green betoken? If she was of the Ring Fire's party, she would have been dressed in red or gold. If she was a wizard, then in blue of some hue. But why *green*? She glanced around at M'Kinnik, who was seated at Rowanne's right hand. The man was smirking, as if he was Fleabag with a particularly delicately flavoured dish of fish. So *he* knew who the stranger was, and he was delighted! How could this stranger please both the Ring Fire *and* the wizards?

In fact, the Ring Fire was burning in Gemma's hand so brightly, she had to hide the light under the sleeves of her robe, in case she was accused of making a move before the trial had formally begun. She moved aside for the stranger to take her place.

From under the veil an almost-familiar voice spoke: 'My Lady Chancellor, as I am not versed in the ways of this trial, please take the first turn.'

M'Kinnik leaned over to Rowanne and whispered. Rowanne nodded and raised her arms. At that second, although it had been midday when they had entered the hall, everything went as dark as midnight. But there was no panic, just silence. All that broke it was an occasional shuffle of a foot or a sniff or a cough. No one spoke or moved. The waiting grew intense; it was obvious that the wizards were waiting for a magical reply from the Ring Fire's Champion. Gemma was getting nervous. At last,

186

after what can only have been a few moments, but felt like at least an hour, Gemma stepped forward to touch the stranger on the shoulder. 'Are you all right?'

'Yes,' came the reply. 'I need the King's Ring. Will he give it to me?'

'I would,' came the reply, out of the dark, 'but it never comes off, even if I want it to.'

'Try it,' Gemma whispered urgently, hoping that this wasn't a trick of M'Kinnik's to get the Ring.

Phelan tugged, and with a gasp of amazement, he found the Ring came loose with ease. 'Where are you, Champion?' he asked.

'Here,' came a familiar voice out of the blackness.

In the dark, without the deception of appearances, Gemma realized who the stranger was. '*Kern?*' she whispered in amazement.

'Hush!' the Champion warned. 'I'll explain later.'

Then, with a few shufflings, the Ring changed hands. The girl held it high, and the warm glow at the heart of the great opal rose into the air to about the height of Phelan. Then suddenly she dashed it to the floor. There was a flash of blinding light from the Fire at the Ring's heart, leaving a shimmering circle at their feet.

The wizards gasped and hid their eyes as the blaze slowly grew to be brighter than several torches.

Rowanne stood and faced the Flame, eyes wide open. For a second, Gemma thought her old friend was about to run towards it, seeking refuge. But she did not. Instead she also raised an arm and hid her face. With the other hand, she made a fist, and pointed at the floor with her index finger. All at once,

187

the floor was seething with what seemed to be snakes slithering towards them from all sides. With a short word of command from Rowanne, the creatures began twisting and twining themselves around Gemma and Phelan's legs, then they caught onto Kern's robe and found Fleabag last of all.

The cat hissed and spat as fiercely as any serpent, as he bit and scratched at their hard, shiny scales. But it did no good. The creatures had other plans. As each one came close to one of the friends, instead of spitting venom, their eyes swelled bigger and bigger, shining with images and memories of evil things half forgotten.

'Close your eyes, don't look!' Phelan warned.

'What *are* they?' Gemma panted, as one snake began to tighten itself around her left arm, reminding her all the while of an evil palace cook with a raised rolling pin.

'They are our worst nightmares!' Phelan gulped. 'They have no power over you unless you let them. Don't let them take hold, and you'll be all right! They can't hurt you unless you let them.'

A mocking sneer came from M'Kinnik as he pointed at Kern with his wand. 'Go on, *girl*, play your fiddle. Charm the snakes as you tried to do to us. You might even find it works this time!' and he laughed a hard, sharp sound.

Stepping free of the snakes into the light of the Ring Fire which glowed warmly from Phelan's Ring on the floor, the Champion shook off her green veil and pulled the silk from her bundle, revealing her violin. She put the instrument on her shoulder and lifted the bow.

'Kern! No!' Gemma shouted. 'Don't do it!'

'Silence!' roared M'Kinnik, as he flung another nightmare in Gemma's direction. It caught her around the neck and wrapped itself around her mouth so she couldn't speak for dread that the Ring Fire might go out.

The girl turned and looked at Gemma with a steady gaze, then she lifted the bow over the strings and held it there for a long moment. Then with a sudden flick of her left wrist, she swung the violin around, smashed it over M'Kinnik's head, and rammed the bow into his chest.

'Whatever is wizard-blue will ultimately betray you,' she said, quite calmly. 'Or so your Chancellor told me once.'

M'Kinnik sank to the ground groaning, and was immediately surrounded by three or four nightmare-creatures. Once they had caught his gaze he was helpless, drowning in a sea of memories and terrors.

The surrounding wizards dived forward to grab the Champion, but she took a deep breath and began to sing. The sound made her enemies stagger back, with their fingers in their ears. At first it was a sound without words that seemed to float in the air, conjuring images of the sea and wind, making the listener float like a gull under a golden-red sunset. Then the voice fell and became dark and green as the depth of the sea, with purples and fresh, wholesome blues swirling around in the listeners' minds.

The wizards' evil was weakened by these thoughts of good things, crumbling the power of the spell and making the nightmare creatures slither away from the Ring Fire's friends. The wizards muttered and cursed, complaining that their ears and eyes hurt, but the singer did not stop for a second. Instead she swung her voice up again to sound like green grass and wild, tangled flowers, a song made from the old woman's tapestry. Needing something to devour, the creatures began to spread amongst their masters instead, staring into their too-blue eyes and feeding on their terror.

But, with strengthened resolve, a few wizards managed to turn the snake-like creatures back towards the Champion and her friends again. And this time the dream-serpents were bigger and angrier than before.

Gemma found herself facing a snake with a wide-open mouth and dagger-like fangs. It told her her parents had never loved her. Phelan faced a beast with a sickly blue-forked tongue that licked and flickered over his face, telling him he would end up betraying Gemma. Kern's singing began to hesitate as a thick pair of pythons began to twine about her, dragging her arms down, telling her her hands were useless and she would never play a violin again.

But then Phelan's rich voice suddenly joined in with Kern's, taking up the song, making up new words, developing the melody as he went along. And Gemma managed to pull the pythons away from Kern, so she could strengthen her voice, weaving in and out of Phelan's themes.

Although the song kept the nightmare creatures at bay, it was not enough to win the trial. Gemma tried to think, but she could not. They could not keep this up for ever. They seemed to be in a sort of stalemate with nightmare evenly matched against singing. There seemed to be no way to break free from what was happening. If only they could find the Ring's End, whatever it was, she had a feeling that everything would be all right. The Fire Giver, if that was who the old lady was, had promised that they already had everything they needed to win the Challenge, and the answer was under Phelan's nose. But the semi-darkness and the hissing snakes and the impossibility of her situation crowded in on her until she felt claustrophobic and hopeless.

Suddenly Gemma realized a nightmare-snake had softly wound its way around her head. She tugged it off and threw it to the ground. And as she did so, something caught her eye.

Phelan's Ring, glowing and alive on the floor, was *not* a complete circle. How could she have been so stupid! The Ring had a beginning *and* an end – at the Great Opal! It *had* been under Phelan's nose the whole time!

She nudged Kern who looked down in the direction of Gemma's pointing and nodded. She stopped singing and whispered. 'Of course! I know what to do now. If everything goes wrong, jump into the Ring Fire at the Ring's End!'

'But how can we? It's only tiny!' Gemma looked confused.

Kern grabbed Gemma's hand and looked her straight in the eyes. 'You asked me to trust you once, now it's your turn. Trust me!'

26

The Ring's End

Gemma looked at the King's Ring lying at her feet.
It was the only part of the floor they could see; the
rest was filled with writhing snake-like creatures.
But how could they all step into such a tiny thing?
She opened her mouth to object, then shut it again.
For she remembered how Kern had led them
through stranger places than this as they wandered
the halls and corridors of the University, folding
space and even time, then expanding it again as they
slipped between dimensions.

But she had little time to wonder, for Kern had
stepped forward to stand amongst the snakes and
face Rowanne, face to face in the eerie mixture of
Ring Fire and baleful blue light. Kern pulled herself
up to her full height and spoke so everyone could
hear. 'My Lady Rowanne, Chancellor of All Wizards.
Do you know why I of all people was sent to fetch
you from Harflorum?'

The Chancellor shrugged. 'Because no one would
know you were from Porthwain, I suppose.'

'No, M'Kinnik sent me because he suspected that
I was the old Chancellor's third daughter, not his

seventh son. This meant that I harboured the greatest powers possible in a wizard. You and this so-called Challenge were just the bait to draw me out.'

'How dare you!' Rowanne slammed her hand on the table at her side. 'Your father may have been fooled into thinking you were a boy, but you didn't deceive everybody. It is true we tested your magical powers today, but you failed! You may be the Chancellor's third daughter, but the blood of the Hill People has made you weak. You aren't a powerful enough wizard to defeat me! You're nothing but a guttersnipe and guttersnipes belong in the gutter!' Rowanne was brilliant blue with rage, and looked as if she was about to explode.

Gemma winced, remembering her own days of begging in the street markets. She was about to say something in Kern's defence, but Rowanne had only paused for a moment's breath. There was no interrupting her.

'Tell them, M'Kinnik!' Rowanne went on. 'Tell them the truth, that I am the greatest wizard ever, and I was chosen from ages past, and as the Ring Fire ignored me and would not acknowledge my greatness, the Blue Magic made me its own to be the great lady I was destined to be.'

'Ah!' whispered Phelan, 'So *that* was at the bottom of it all, wounded pride. That figures!'

But M'Kinnik, slumped in his chair, nursing his sore head and chest, just laughed as loudly as he dare without causing himself pain. 'No, Lady Rowanne, I'm afraid our little girl there is quite right. Here she is, our real future, the greatest of all wizards. She's masqueraded as a boy these thirteen years. I always suspected, but her father forbade me to have anything to do with her. He proclaimed the baby outcast and untouchable when the midwife showed him a boy child.

'Domnall guessed, though. He put that fiddle in her hands and we all knew. No ordinary mortal could play like that. But Domnall had his own plans to be great, so he taught his little 'brother' very carefully, using spells disguised as music. He was training her to be great. Under him, of course. But no one can be greater than a Chancellor's third daughter. And look what happened to him! Defeated by that so-called Fire Wielder on Spider Island!

'But I kept believing in you, child...' The fat, sour-faced wizard stepped forward to pat Kern on her cheek. 'Uncle M'Kinnik's always been *very* fond of you...'

Kern recoiled at his touch, and plucked another serpent from her skirt. 'That's not true. You've always hated me!' she glowered. 'You were just using me for your own ends! You thought if I was the third daughter you could keep me out of sight in the kitchens, and use me secretly to enhance your own powers. You didn't even want *me* to know who I was!'

M'Kinnik grinned, although he was obviously still in pain, ' That's right, my dear,' he said. 'You *are* clever, aren't you?'

Then he turned to Rowanne. 'But the beauty of my plan was that if the "boy" Kern did not turn out to be the great wizard we had all hoped for, we still had you, our pretty blue puppet who has absorbed far more of the blue magic than any human can stand. You will grow old and physically weak, but magically very powerful, and live in our nice warm

University for many a thousand years, doing our bidding and being adored by us all.'

Rowanne had indeed of late been feeling a little stiff and drained, and was no longer the fine-featured young woman she once had been. But she was still stronger than most men.

She grasped the wounded M'Kinnik by his robes and dragged him to stand in front of her. 'How dare you? How dare you treat me like this? *I* am the Chancellor! You obey me and you do not mock me! Do you understand?'

But her shouts fell on deaf ears, for not only M'Kinnik, but the whole company of wizards were all laughing until their sides hurt.

'You've been offered a wooden bone, Rowanne,' Fleabag smirked. 'You were the bait and the catch, all at the same time. Pity. You really didn't deserve it!'

In a flash, Rowanne tugged off her wizard's cloak and drew out a small sword she still carried secretly. With a swift slash, M'Kinnik lay dead at her feet, and a few more of the senior wizards followed.

With one hand, she warded off spells that were flung at her; with the other, she slashed and cut, killing and maiming more and more with every move. The crowd pressed in around her. Phelan stood guard over the Ring, which was still glowing on the floor, and Gemma held the Ring Fire high in her hands. Fleabag moved to take his stand next to Rowanne, his old enemy, and much-loved friend.

'Quick, everyone,' Rowanne called over her shoulder, 'go to the Ring's End. It's your only chance! It may be too late for me, but it's not for you. Flee to the Fire Giver!'

Phelan took Gemma by the shoulders and, before she could object, pushed her through the opal gateway in the narrow band of gold on the floor. Once again, Gemma felt a twinge of uncertainty about how on earth she could step into such a tiny space. But as they moved towards it, the Ring's stone grew huge and opened wide. She could not let her mind question it. She just had to move! Phelan was right behind her and Kern tumbled after them.

The little room on the other side was circular, with tall lancet windows all around. It was the right room, but it was empty and grey.

'Light the Ring Fire in the grate!' Kern ordered. 'Do it now, to prevent the wizards from following us through.'

'But what about Rowanne and Fleabag?' Gemma gasped, as she held out her hands in the empty grate, watching the rise of the golden flames which burned nothing.

'They'll come when they can,' Phelan assured her.

Outside, in the hall, Rowanne was growing tired as she fought off the Blue Magic and tried to swing her sword at the same time. Beside her, the noble Fleabag cut and clawed at the legs and ankles of every one who came within reach. He ignored the spells and curses that bought illusions of huge black rats with yellow eyes and infected teeth charging across the floor at him. He concentrated and used his sixth sense that told him they were not real. The wizards did not know his real name, so they could not put spells on him, but that was not their only weapon.

For suddenly, Fleabag found himself face to face with a terrible sight – one he had thought he would never have to face again; the sight of the axe swung at his beloved Queen Sophia, so many years ago, when he was a kitten and she was not much older than Gemma.

The assassin was blue-robed and evil-eyed, with breath that smelled of dog sweat on a hot day. Once again, Fleabag relived jumping to try to fend off the blow, and watched his own back leg spin away from him as it caught the blade.

The pain was as real as it had been on that day. It seared and burned him to the bone, and he felt faint with the agony of it, throbbing and tearing into his fur, unyielding, causing him to vomit.

Then suddenly, as he tried to tell himself it was just another nightmare, he realized it wasn't. Before him stood that same ancient wizard with a blue cloak and evil eyes, leaning over him with raised hands. But, as before, he was not wielding a spell. He carried another, and a very real axe!

'No!' yelled Rowanne, as she flung herself across Fleabag, catching the second blow on the side of her own head. 'You'll be all right. I'll take you to the Ring's End,' she gasped as she fell. But the wizard took another swipe. 'We'll have no black cats or Fire Maidens in here!' he sneered, and kicked Fleabag out of Rowanne's arms and across the floor.

Rowanne rolled back and grabbed Fleabag's warm, limp body. Then, twisting to her knees, she turned and sprang through the Opal into the fire-grate of the circular room beyond.

'Oh thank goodness, you're all right!' Gemma laughed, catching up a live and purring Fleabag and hugging him.

Then Rowanne got to her feet and pushed her dark brown hair out of her eyes. She laughed as she looked around her. Everyone was safe. 'Oh, thank goodness you're all right. I'm so sorry for all the trouble I've caused you!' she cried, as she hugged them all in turn.

'Are you all here now?' asked a voice behind them. And there, sitting next to the fire, was the old woman in her dress of flowers, once again doing her tapestry. 'My sewing is done for today,' she said, placing her needle and silks into a small box by her side.

'Fleabag, jump up onto my lap, and Rowanne, open the windows will you? All of them.'

27

Night Wanderer

As Rowanne opened the windows a warm, summer breeze filled the room.

'Now you must all choose,' said the old woman. 'Whichever window you go through will be your future. There will be no way back, for the place you knew as Porthwain is now gone. Since you left, which in your time was hours ago, the wizards have destroyed each other and everything that went with the town. Your men escaped, Phelan. They are well on their way home. But there truly is nothing left of the University or of the Blue Magic.'

Gemma picked up Fleabag and carried him to where Phelan was leaning out of the first window and saw Harflorum, with all its bright colours and happy streets. The King was smiling. 'I've missed it,' he said. 'Harflorum really is home, even with the Prime Minister and all his fussiness.'

Then Gemma moved to the next window and saw her beloved cottage in the rocks with Fleabag's sons, Hereward and Rufus, and the lonely hills that she loved so much.

At the next window Rowanne was looking out at

Erbwenneth and a party of soldiers going out to patrol the forest roads around the city. At their head was her younger brother, Alawn, with Aidan acting as his squire. The young prince sat very straight on his horse, and looked a good and honest man.

'They don't really need me there, any more, do they?' Rowanne asked sadly, as she leaned against the stone mullions.

The old woman shook her head and smiled. 'No, my dear, they don't. But you did a good job of making Erbwenneth safe and quiet. Your people will remember you with love.'

Rowanne blushed a deep pink. 'I don't really deserve that,' she muttered, and hung her head.

'No one ever gets what they really deserve, thank goodness,' Fleabag commented as he jumped down from Gemma's arms and walked along each windowledge in turn, peering and sniffing the breezes that came in from each direction, and making rude insinuations about the quality of mouse and shrew to be had at each place.

Then he jumped onto the old woman's flower-covered lap and purred as she stroked him until his long fur gleamed, soft and smooth, under her fine fingers.

Kern alone did not go to any of the windows. Instead, she sat on the hearthrug, clasping her knees and looking glum. 'What's the matter?' asked Gemma, sitting beside her and giving her a hug. 'You can go anywhere you like from here. You're free at last.'

'But where's my mother?' Kern muttered miserably. 'I thought she'd be here!'

The old woman laughed gently. 'Well, you haven't looked very hard, have you?'

Kern glanced up and gasped, for leaning into the room from the last window was Claire, looking well and happy, and dressed in a gown so green it might have been woven from spring fields.

Kern jumped up and ran across the room, intending to jump out to her mother, but Claire had already swung her legs into the room. The two laughed and cried and hugged until they were quite exhausted. At last Claire sat down, with her daughter cuddled very close to her side. She looked around at Kern's friends. 'I have dreamed of you people, I am sure of it,' she smiled and held out a hand to them. 'But it was a strange dream. It was as if I could see you through a great milky white stone with a warm fire making your faces glow. I feel as if I have been asleep for ever. I think I must have dreamed a whole world.'

'In a way, you have,' Kern smiled. 'I will tell you all about it later. But what happened to you? When I came back from Harflorum, you were gone.'

Claire shrugged. 'I really don't know how I got here. M'Kinnik told me you had run away and wouldn't come back. I didn't believe him, and I wanted to go looking for you. I remember trying to flee the city one night, with guards trying to catch me. I thought I was hopelessly cornered and I slipped inside a tiny doorway. I remember finding myself in a room much like this one, small and round, but bare and cold. I hid at the back of a great stone fireplace and held my breath. I remember the door opening, but nothing else.'

'The Ring Fire kept you and protected you,' Phelan smiled. 'But although I know the Fire Giver cares about all her people, why were you so important to M'Kinnik? Why was the old Chancellor so keen for you to have his baby daughter?'

Claire smiled. 'I am one of the Hill People. We have farmed the lower slopes of the mountains for many years, though we have been driven into poverty and near hopelessness by the wizards for a very long time. My people were wise and gentle. Above all we were singers, and our music was strong against the Blue Magic. But, one by one, we were killed or trapped or ruined in one way or another. We have forgotten our ancient arts; now we keep the few songs we do know a closely guarded secret. But even this prevented the wizards' power from spreading any further north.

'The old Chancellor had been told that the only way to defeat us was to have a powerful third daughter by a Hill woman, and raise her to the ways of the Blue Magic. He had foreseen that such a wizard could bring about the defeat of her own people if she was taught magic from an early age.

'My family was so poor, I was taken by the University bailiff instead of farm rent, but I did not know the old Chancellor's designs. When my daughter was born, the midwife, who was one of the Hill People as well, hid the child, and replaced it with a new-born baby boy she had smuggled into my room in a basket of linen. Even I did not know my child was a girl until I was well enough to wash and care for her myself. By that time, the Chancellor had disowned me, and I was left to scrub and work in the kitchens like any other slave.

'But this is my daughter, Saoirse, which means "Freedom" in the old tongue. You'd probably pronounce it "Sorsha". I called her "Kern" and dressed her as a boy, until she was old enough to understand the truth.'

'But,' Gemma butted in, 'If you are a third daughter, Saoirse, you have great magical powers?'

Saoirse laughed. 'Supposedly. But I despise the wizards' magic and all it stands for. I chose not to take my father's inheritance, but to follow my mother's ways instead. I soon realized I had power in my music, but I always tried to use it for good. I want people to be free like the wind, and the wild flowers of the green hills. As you might say, the way the Fire Giver intended us to be. I learned how to listen to all sorts of living creatures, and to sing their songs. I found I often knew things: where someone is hurting, and how to heal it, or what is causing a grief and why. Many people call that magic, but I'm sure it is simply listening and watching. It is how we are all meant to be.'

Phelan and Gemma exchanged glances. 'I can understand that,' Gemma admitted. 'But what had you planned to do next? You couldn't pretend to be a boy for ever.'

'That was the difficult bit. I knew I had to leave the University by the time I was about thirteen. But I would not – in fact I could not – leave without my mother. She is all I have. Where could I go without her? I couldn't leave her to be kicked around for the rest of her life; she is a wonderful person! We planned to travel the world and sing to earn a living. But she was kept a virtual slave here. Now we know that M'Kinnik suspected us, it all makes sense. He knew if she was here I would never leave. He was just waiting to see what happened to me as time passed.'

Fleabag sniffed at Saoirse's hand. 'You never smelled like a boy – I assumed you just didn't like dressing in girls' clothes. Why didn't the wizards just smell you?'

'Humans can't smell things like you can,' Phelan explained. 'Go on, Saoirse.'

The girl shrugged. 'I can see now that the Challenge to you was all an elaborate trap to catch me out. M'Kinnik sent me to find the carrier of the Blue Magic. He promised me that if I did it, my mother and I would both be free. It was too good an opportunity to miss – we could leave together – but we should have suspected something. It was all too easy.'

'But how was the Challenge a trap?' Gemma asked.

'The wizards knew that as I became a teenager my powers would grow. They hoped that if I were faced with the Blue Magic at its strongest, I would try using it and allow myself to become one of them. They knew I didn't want to, but they hoped to force my hand. When I came to Harflorum, I never wanted to have anything to do with wizards or Kings or Fire Wielders *or* black cats: I hated you all. I wanted to find Rowanne and then run away. I *wanted* her to be Chancellor. Anyone but me!

'But I met you and your Ring Fire and realized that hating and running away wouldn't help anyone. I knew I was the only one strong enough to be your Champion. I had enough magical power at my disposal today to defeat the wizards – all of them at once, if I chose. But I didn't choose. To fight them

204

with their sort of magic would have been to become like them. There was a much simpler and stronger way. All I had to do was to face the wizards with the truth about themselves – to show them their own worst nightmare; that I did *not* want them! Truth is always stronger than any spells.'

Rowanne shuddered at this. 'And it worked,' she put in. 'I'm sorry and I'm very grateful. I just couldn't see what I was doing!'

Gemma squeezed Rowanne's hand. 'And I'm sorry for not being kinder to you. I'm glad it's all over now,' she said.

'And it's time for you all to go home!' put in the old woman. 'Make your choices, for when the sun goes down, it will be another day for other heroes and other dreams.'

Gemma hugged Phelan and Saoirse. Then she stood by the window that overlooked the cottage in the rocks. 'I want to go home. Thanks for everything. Come and see me if you are ever on my road.'

The girl smiled. 'Thank you, too. Your home is not far from my grandfather's. I may well come and visit one day.'

Phelan shook Saoirse's hand. He smiled. 'I still owe you a violin, and you still owe me an evening's playing. You are always welcome in Harflorum.'

She nodded. 'Thanks. Musicians are treated well in your palace. Mother and I will take you up on your offer, especially if the winter gets cold!'

'Make sure you do.'

Then she turned to Fleabag who just purred and rolled over for his tummy to be tickled. 'Remember, no more cat-gut!' he growled.

'I promise,' she laughed, as she took her mother's hand, and disappeared through the window that looked south.

Gemma put her feet over the ledge that took her to the mountains. 'I presume you're staying here by the fire?' she asked Fleabag.

'Of course. I know where I'm well off,' he grinned.

Gemma picked the cat up and rubbed her face in his smooth, soft fur, wiping a tear away as she did so. 'Bye, you disreputable old ratter. Be good!'

Fleabag sniffed derisively. 'Am I ever anything else?' But the sniff sounded a little odd, and he hid behind the old woman's skirts.

Gemma tried to sound cheerful. 'Are *you* coming, Rowanne?' she asked.

The Princess shook her head. 'I'm not going back. I think I must stay here now. Maybe the Lady Fire Giver has work for me to do.'

'Indeed, I do,' the old woman smiled, as she rose from her chair by the fire, and stretched out her arms to pull the dark blue silk of the night across the skies. 'We all have much to do now. Even Fleabag. But I do hope he will be happy with me.'

The cat reappeared, having found his composure. He spread his whiskers wide and stalked over to the fireside where he sat on the rug with the warmth on his back. 'Why ever shouldn't I be happy here? This is heaven!'

The old lady laughed as she lit the moon. 'I don't have any fleas here. You will have nothing to scratch and moan about, and you will have to use your real name again.'

'What *is* your real name, Fleabag?' Gemma asked.

'Surely it's safe to tell it here?'

'Night-Wanderer Moon-Eyes,' the cat replied, as he jumped onto the window ledge. Then he sat down and began washing his fourth leg in the cool of the evening breeze. 'Send Tabitha and the kittens my love, won't you?' he called as Gemma and Phelan climbed through the windows into their own places, and disappeared into the shadows.

Only the gleam of Fleabag's golden eyes was left, glowing in the sable night.

All Lion books are available from your local bookshop, or can be ordered via our website or from Marston Book Services. For a free catalogue, showing the complete list of titles available, please contact:

Customer Services
Marston Book Services
PO Box 269
Abingdon
Oxon
OX14 4YN

Tel: 01235 465522
Fax: 01235 465555

Our website can be found at:
www.lion-publishing.co.uk